W9-ARO-795

ILLUSTRATED CLASSICS

Huckleberry Finn

Mark Twain

Adapted by
Bookmatrix Ltd

Edited by
Claire Black

Published by

Huckleberry Finn

Mark Twain

First Published in 2006 •
ISBN 1-84577-091-9 • Printed in India

Contents

CHAPTER I

Life at Widow Douglas' Place

You won't know about me without reading a book called The Adventures of Tom Sawyer. But it doesn't matter. Mr. Mark Twain wrote the book and what he wrote in it was mostly true. The way the book winds up is this: my friend Tom Sawyer and I found the money that some robbers hid in a cave. It made us rich! Both of us got six thousand dollars each. Judge Thatcher put the money out at interest, and it fetched us a dollar a month each all the year round.

Widow Douglas adopted me. She took a liking to me. Maybe she was kind of grateful after Tom and I saved her from the robbers. But it was rough living in her house 'cause she tried to civilize me. When I couldn't stand it any longer I ran away and got into my old rags again. I was free and happy then.

But Tom Sawyer soon hunted me up. He said he was going to start a band of robbers, and I might join only if I would go back to the widow and start leading a respectable life. So, I went back.

The widow cried over me, and called me a 'poor lost lamb' and a lot of other names too. Then she put me in new clothes; and once again I began to feel all cramped up and started sweating all over.

Then there was the widow's sister, Miss Watson, a slim old maid wearing goggles who had just come to stay with her. She right away took an interest in me and tried to teach me how to read and spell. She worked me real hard for an hour or so, till I could stand it no longer and started getting fidgety. Then she would say, "Don't put your feet up there, Huckleberry;" and, "Don't scrunch up like that, Huckleberry—sit up straight;" and pretty soon she would say, "Don't gap and stretch like that, Huckleberry—why don't you try to behave?" She kept pecking at me till I was quite tired and lonesome.

One night, after I had finished my lessons, I went up to my room with a piece of candle, and put it on the table. The house was silent. I tried to think of something cheery, but it was of no use. I felt so lonely and unhappy that I wished I was dead. I could see the stars shining, and hear the rustle of leaves. Then I heard an owl hooting far and a dog crying about. I became depressed and scared, and wished I had some company.

After a long time I heard the town clock

striking twelve. And, pretty soon, I heard a twig snap down in the dark among the trees; something was moving about there. I sat still and listened. I could just barely hear a 'me-yow, me-yow' below my window.

It was a signal!

I whispered back, "Me-yow!" and then climbing out of the window, I slipped down to the ground. And, sure enough, there was Tom Sawyer waiting for me!

Tom and I went tiptoe along a path amongst the trees, stooping down so that the branches wouldn't scrape our heads. Suddenly, I fell over a root and made a noise. Miss Watson's slave, Jim who was sitting at the kitchen door got up and said, "Who that?" Both of us crouched down and lay still. Jim stood listening for some more sound for a while, and then he came and stood right between us. We remained where we were, as still as a mouse. Suddenly, my ankle started itching. But I dared not scratch it. Then,

my ear began to itch, and next, my back. It seemed as if I'd die if I couldn't scratch!

However, soon Jim started speaking, "Who is you? Where is you? Well, I know what I is going to do; I is going to sit down here till I hear it again." Then Jim sat down on the ground between Tom and me. He leaned his back against a tree, and stretched out his legs till one of them almost touched one of mine.

And then my nose started to itch. It itched in one place, then another, and then yet another, till tears came into my eyes. My nose was itching in eleven different places now and I thought I couldn't stand it any longer! Thankfully, Jim started breathing heavily and began to snore. And pretty soon, I was comfortable again.

At this moment Tom made a sign to me and we crept away on our hands and knees. After a while, we reached the top of the hill on the other side of the house. We found Jo Harper and Ben Rogers, and two or three more of the boys hid in the old tan-yard. So we unhitched a small boat, pulled down the river to the big scar on the hillside and went ashore. There, Tom took us to a clump of bushes and showed us an opening in the hill, right within the thickest part of the bushes. We crawled in on our hands and knees for about two hundred yards till we found ourselves in a kind of cold and damp room.

"Now, we'll start this gang of robbers and call it Tom Sawyer's Gang," declared Tom, "Everybody who wants to join has got to take an oath, and write his name in blood." Everybody was willing. So we lit candles and Tom read us the oath that he had written, taken mostly from robber books and pirate stories. It swore every boy to stick to the gang, and never tell any of the secrets. If any gang member told the secrets he must be killed, his carcass burnt up and the ashes scattered all around, his name blotted off the list with blood, and forgotten forever.

Everybody said it was a real beautiful oath. Some suggested it would be good to kill the FAMILIES of boys that told the secrets. Tom said it was a good idea, so he took a pencil and wrote it in. Then Ben Rogers argued over what my role in the gang will be, because I did not have a family for the boys to kill, in case I reveal any of the gang's secrets. And although I did have a father, he was nowhere to be found these days. Well, nobody could think of any thing to do but to rule me out of the gang. I was almost ready to cry, but all at once I thought of a way. I offered them Miss Watson – they could kill her.

Everybody said, "Oh, she'll do. Huck can come in."

All of us then signed an oath in blood to join the band.

Little Tommy Barnes was asleep until now. When they waked him up he was scared, and

cried, and said he wanted to go home to his mother, and didn't want to be a robber any more.

So they all made fun of him, and called him cry-baby. That made him mad, and he said he would go straight and tell all the secrets. But Tom gave him five cents to keep quiet and said we would meet next week. We elected Tom Sawyer first captain and Jo Harper second captain of the gang, and then started for home. I climbed up the shed and crept into my window just before day was breaking. My new clothes were all greased up and muddy, and I was dog-tired.

I got a good scolding in the morning from Miss Watson because of my clothes. But, Widow Douglas didn't scold me but only cleaned off the grease and mud from my clothes, and looked so sorry that I thought I would behave awhile if I could.

Our gang played robber now and then for

about a month, and then all the boys got tired of it. Actually, we hadn't robbed anybody, but just pretended. And so, pretty soon, our gang fell apart.

CHAPTER 2

Pap Returns

Three or four months went by, and it was winter now. I had been to school most of the time and could spell and read and write just a little, and could say the multiplication table up to six times seven, that is thirty-five.

I don't think I could get further than that even if I were to live forever!

At first, I just hated school. But, by and by I

got sort of used to it. I was getting sort of used to the widow's ways, too. I liked the old ways best, but I was getting to like the new ones too, just a bit. The widow said I was improving slowly but surely, and doing very satisfactorily. She said she wasn't ashamed of me.

One morning, during breakfast I upset the salt-shaker. I felt sure that this was going to bring me bad luck. Feeling worried and shaky and wondering what it was going to be, I went down to the front garden and climbed over the stile.

There was an inch of new snow on the ground, and I saw somebody's tracks. Whoever it was, had come up from the quarry, stood around the stile for sometime, and then went on around the garden fence. It was funny he hadn't come in, after standing around so. I couldn't make anything out of it. It was very curious and I stooped down to look at the tracks carefully. Then I noticed something else.

The left boot-heel had a cross mark made with big nails, to fend off the devil. I knew it at once: it was Pap's boot!

I was up in a second and running down the hill. I looked over my shoulder every now and then, but I didn't see anybody. I reached Judge Thatcher's place as quickly as I could get there.

"Why, my boy, you are all out of breath!" he said, on seeing me so. "Did you come for your interest?"

"No, sir," I said, "is there some for me?"

"Oh, yes, a half-yearly interest came last night – of over a hundred and fifty dollars. Quite a fortune for you! You had better let me invest it along with your six thousand, because if you take it you'll spend it."

"No, sir," I replied. "I don't want it at all – nor the six thousand, neither. I want to give it to you – the six thousand and everything."

Judge Thatcher looked surprised. He couldn't figure me out. "Why, what do you

mean by it, my boy?" he said.

"Please take it, and don't ask me anything," I said, "then I won't have to tell lies."

He thought for a while, and then said, "Oho-o! You want to SELL all your property to me—not give it."

Then he wrote something on a paper and read it over, and paid me a dollar and I signed the paper and left. That night, I lit my candle, went up to my room and shut the door. As I turned around... there sat Pap in my room!

I used to be scared of Pap: he used to beat me so hard. I think I was scared of him now, too; but in a minute I realised that I was mistaken. After the first jolt at seeing him so unexpectedly in my room was over, I understood that I wasn't so much afraid of him after all!

He was almost fifty, and he looked it. His hair was long, tangled and greasy. It was black, not grey. So were his long, mixed-up whiskers. His face was white, just like the belly of a fish and one could see his eyes shining through like he was behind vines. He was sitting with one ankle resting on the other knee; the boot on that foot was busted, and two of his toes stuck through, and he worked them now and then. His clothes were all in rags and his old black slouch hat was lying on the floor.

I stood looking at him and he sat there looking at me, with his chair tilted back a little. I noticed the window was up; that meant he had climbed in by the shed. Pap kept on looking at me all over.

"Smart clothes...very smart clothes," he said, after a while, "You think you've become some hot-shot, don't you?"

"Maybe I am, maybe I am not," I said.

"Don't you give me any o' your lip," said he. "You've got into great many fancy things since I been away. You're educated, too, they say. Who said you might meddle with such foolishness, hey?"

"The widow told me."

"Well, I'll teach her how to meddle. And look here, you drop that school, you hear? None of the family could read. I won't stand it. And they say you're rich."

"They lie."

"I've been in town two days, and I haven't heard nothing but about you bein' rich. That's why I came. You get me that money tomorrow, I want it."

"I have got only a dollar, and I want that too."

"It doesn't make any difference what you want it for; you just shell it out."

Pap took my dollar and then went down town to get some whisky. Next day he was drunk, and he went to Judge Thatcher and bully ragged him, and tried to make him give up my money. But Pap couldn't, and then he swore he'd make the law force the judge.

The judge and the widow went to the court

to take me away from Pap and let one of them be my guardian. But a new judge had just come, and he didn't know the old man; so he said courts mustn't interfere and separate families; and that he'd rather not take a child away from its father.

The court's decision pleased the old man. Pap said if I didn't raise some money for him he'd thrash me till I was black and blue. I borrowed three dollars from Judge Thatcher, and Pap took it, got drunk and went shouting and cursing all over town, beating a tin pan till almost midnight. Then he got jailed for a week.

CHAPTER 3

A Kidnapping and a Murder Plot

Well, pretty soon Pap went for Judge Thatcher in the courts to make him give up that money. He went for me, too, for not stopping school. He caught me a couple of times and thrashed me.

The law trial was a slow business and it looked like it would never begin. So, every now and then, I'd borrow two or three dollars from the judge for Pap, to keep him away from thrashing me. And every time Pap got money, he got drunk.

Pap started hanging around the widow's too much and so she told him that if he didn't stop it, she would make trouble for him. Pap got very angry at this and said he would show who Huck Finn's boss was!

So, he looked out for me one day during spring and caught me. Then he took me up the river in a small boat, and crossed over to the Illinois shore. Here it was woody and there weren't any houses but an old log hut. All around the hut the wood was so thick you couldn't find it if you didn't know where it was. It was an old log cabin.

Pap carefully locked the door and never left my side. So, I never got a chance to run off. He had a gun which I think he had stolen, and we fished and hunted, and that was what we lived on. Every once in a while he locked me in and

went down to the store three miles away by the ferry, and traded fish and game for whisky. He fetched it home, got drunk and beat me sometimes, and had a good time.

Two months passed by and my clothes became all ragged and dirty. But on the whole it was sort of a jolly and lazy life, and I didn't have to go to school any longer. But, by and by Pap got too handy with his belt after he got drunk, and I couldn't stand it. I was covered with bruises and belt marks. He was going away a good deal too, and locking me in.

Once, he locked me in and was gone three days. I was dreadfully lonesome. I judged he had got drowned, and I wasn't ever going to get out any more. I was scared.

So, I made up my mind that I would fix up some way to leave from there. I had tried to get out of that cabin many a time, but I couldn't find any way. There wasn't a window big enough for a dog to get away; the chimney was too narrow;

and the door was made of thick solid oak slabs. Pap was pretty careful not to leave a knife or anything in the cabin when he was away. But this time I found something at last; I found an old rusty wood-saw without any handle. I greased it up and went to work. At the far end of the cabin behind a table there was an old horse-blanket, nailed against the logs. I got under the table and raised the blanket, and went to work to saw a section of the big bottom log out – big enough to let me through. Well, it was a long job, but I was getting towards the end of it when I heard Pap's gun in the woods. I got rid of the signs of my work, dropped the blanket and hid my saw. Soon after, Pap came in.

He wasn't in a good humour – so he was his natural self. He said he had been downtown, and everything was going wrong. His lawyer said that Judge Thatcher had managed to put off the trial for a long time. And till the trial ended and the decision was made in their favour, there wouldn't be any money.

What's more, people thought there'd be another trial to get me away from him and make the widow my guardian. And they guessed she would win this time. This made me shake, because I didn't want to go back to the widow's again and be quiet and civilised.

Pap cursed everyone. He said he would like to see the widow get me. He threatened to stow me in a place six or seven mile away, where they might hunt till they dropped but still they couldn't find me.

That made me pretty uneasy again. Pap drank and drank, and tumbled down on his blankets by and by. He groaned and moaned in his sleep.

I thought everything all over. I decided not to stay in one place, but run away and roam across the country, hunt and fish for a living, and get so far away that neither the old man nor the widow could ever find me.

Then I too fell asleep.

Next morning, Pap woke me and said, "Don't lie there all day. Go out and see if there's a fish on the lines for breakfast."

He unlocked the door and I went outside. As I climbed up the riverbank, I saw a canoe drifting ashore. I had an idea.

I jumped into the water, swam out to the canoe, climbed in and paddled her ashore. I had thought of a plan: I'd hide her, and instead of running away to the woods I'd go down the river and camp in one place forever. So, I hid the canoe in a little creek all hung over with vines and willows.

I got back pretty late, and Pap abused me a little for being so slow. But I told him I fell in the river, and that was what made me so long. Then we had breakfast and lay down to sleep.

At about twelve o'clock we went along up the bank. The river water was on the rise and bringing in lots of driftwood. By and by part of a log raft worth ten dollars came along. Both of us brought the log raft ashore. Then, Pap locked me in the cabin, took the raft and the logs to the town to sell it. I judged he wouldn't come back that night. I waited until he had a good start, then I took out my saw. Before Pap had reached the other side of the river, I had finished sawing and climbed out.

I dragged a sack of corn meal to where the canoe was hid and put it in. Then I did the same with bacon, coffee and sugar, all the ammunition, bucket and gourd, a tin cup, my old saw, two blankets, skillet, coffee-pot, fish-lines and matches and many other such things.

Then I took out Pap's shotgun, shot a wild pig and took it to the camp. Then I took the axe and smashed in the door. I put the bleeding pig on the floor. Next, I took an old sack and put a lot of big rocks in it; then starting from the pig I dragged the sack to the door and through the woods down to the river and dumped it in. It now looked as if something had been dragged over the ground. I did wish Tom Sawyer was there to throw in the fancy touches.

Last, I pulled out some of my hair, and bloodied the axe, and flung the axe in the corner. Then I took up the pig and dumped him into the river. Everything looked like someone had hacked his way inside the cabin, killed me, dragged my body and dumped it into the river.

It was nearly dark now. So I dropped the canoe down the river under some willows that hung over the bank, and waited for the moon to rise.

I took a bite to eat and then tried to lay down a plan. I knew people would follow the tracks made by the sack of rocks to the river shore. They would then drag the river for my body, but soon get tired of that and would no longer bother about me. So what I wanted now was a hiding place. I decided to head for Jackson's Island. I knew that island pretty well,

and nobody ever came there.

By then I was pretty tired, and before I knew it, I was asleep.

When I woke up, the moon was shining brightly in the sky. Then, I heard a sound over the water. I peeped through the willow branches and saw Pap returning in a small boat.

I lost no time. Immediately, I jumped into the canoe and pushed off. The canoe floated downstream until it reached the deserted Jackson's Island. I got down on the shore and tied the canoe where nobody could easily see it. Then I sat down on a log nearby the shore, and looked out on the big river and away over to the town, three miles away.

There, I could see three or four lights twinkling. I settled down to get some sleep.

CHAPTER 4

A Surprise and a Lesson

The sun was high up when I awoke. I lay there in the grass, rather comfortable and satisfied. There were big trees all about, and a couple of squirrels chattered to me in a friendly way.

I was feeling very lazy and restful – didn't want to get up and cook breakfast. I was dozing off again, when I heard a deep sound of "boom!" away up the river. I hopped up, and looked out at a hole in the leaves. I saw a bunch of smoke alongside the ferry. And the ferryboat was full of people.

I at once knew what the matter was. They were firing cannon over the water, thinking that it would make my body come to the top.

In a while, the ferry drifted in close. Everybody was on the boat—Pap, and Judge Thatcher, and Bessie Thatcher, and Jo Harper, and Tom Sawyer, and his old Aunt Polly and many more. Everybody was talking about the murder.

The captain broke in and said: "The current sets in the closest here. Maybe he's washed ashore and got tangled among the bushes at the water's edge."

At once, all crowded up and leaned over the rails, nearly in my face. I could see them clearly, but they couldn't see me.

After a while, the ferry floated on and went

out of sight. Now, I knew I was all right. Nobody else would come looking for me. I made a nice camp for myself in the thick woods. I made a kind of tent out of my blankets and put my things under it. Then I caught a catfish, and towards sundown, started my campfire and had supper.

When it was dark I sat by my campfire feeling pretty satisfied. But, in a while, it got sort of lonesome. So I listened to the current swashing along, then counted the stars and the logs of wood that drifted by the river.

The next day, I went exploring through the island. I found plenty of strawberries, green summer grapes, and green raspberries and green blackberries.

This went on for three days and nights. On the fourth day, I went along in the deep woods. And suddenly, I bounded right on to the ashes of a campfire. It was still smoking!

My heart jumped up amongst my lungs. I

didn't wait to look further, but went sneaking back as fast as I could. Every now and then, I stopped a second and listened. If I saw a stump, I took it for a man; and if I trod on a stick and broke it, it made me gasp.

When I got to my camp, I got all my things into my canoe again, put out the fire and scattered the ashes around, and then climbed a tree. I think I was up in the tree for two hours; but I didn't see anything. Well, I couldn't stay up there forever; so at last I got down..

By that time it was night, and I was pretty hungry. So I slid out from shore and paddled over to the Illinois bank. I went out in the woods and cooked a supper, when suddenly, I heard a PLUNKETY-PLUNK, PLUNKETY PLUNK.

That night, I didn't sleep much. Every time I woke up, I thought somebody had me by the neck. I decided that I couldn't live in this way for long. I was going to find out who was there on the island with me. I'd find it out or bust.

When it was dawn I slipped off towards where I had made my campfire. But I couldn't seem to find the place. But, by and by I caught a glimpse of fire through the trees. I went towards it, slowly and carefully. When I was close enough I saw a man lying on the ground. He had a blanket around his head, and his head was nearly in the fire.

Pretty soon, he yawned and stretched and threw off the blanket. I could see his face now. It was Miss Watson's Jim!

I was glad to see him. I said, "Hello, Jim!" in great excitement. But Jim bounced up and stared at me with wild eyes.

Then he dropped down on his knees, put his hands together and said, "Don't hurt me—don't! I never done any harm to a ghost."

Well, I wasn't long in making him understand that I wasn't dead. Jim was so glad to see me again that he didn't know what to do. Then I told Jim, "Let's get breakfast. Make up your camp fire good."

We went to where the canoe was tied up. While Jim built a fire, I fetched meal, bacon, coffee, coffee pot, frying pan, sugar and tin cups from the boat. We ate breakfast smoking hot. Then we lay down on the grass to rest. By and by Jim said, "But look here, Huck, who was it that was killed in that shanty if it wasn't you?"

Then I told him the whole thing, and he said it was smart. "But how did you come to be here, Jim, and how'd you get here?" I asked. Jim looked pretty uneasy, and didn't say anything for a minute.

"You wouldn't tell anyone if I told you?" he asked.

When I promised to keep mum, he said, "Huck I—I RUN OFF."

"Jim!" I was awfully shocked. But then I said, "But that doesn't make any difference. I am not going to tell. Now, let's know all about it."

So Jim told me how old Miss Watson always pecked at him and treated him roughly. One night, he overhead Miss Watson telling the widow that she was going to sell him down the river for a good sum of money. The widow tried to talk her out of it. But Jim was so scared that he didn't wait to hear the rest. He decided to escape and ran away to the island. And so, since the past week, Jim had been in hiding.

We decided to look for a safe place to camp in and got to a place I had found in the middle of the island. There, we found a good big cavern in the rock. We hid all our things in the cavern, so that we could rush there if anybody came to the island; then we hid the canoe in a good place nearby.

Next, we began to get ready for dinner and caught some fish. On one side of the cavern door the floor stuck out a little bit, and was flat and a good place to build a fire on. So we built it there and cooked dinner. We spread the blankets inside for a carpet, and ate our dinner in there.

Pretty soon it darkened up, and there was thunder and lightening. It began to rain, and it rained like fury. The river went on rising and rising for ten or twelve days, till at last it was over the banks. One night, we caught a little section of a lumber raft. It was twelve foot wide and about sixteen foot long, and the top stood six or seven inches above water. We could see saw-logs go by in the daylight sometimes, but we let them go; we didn't show ourselves in daylight.

Another night, we saw a two-storey frame house floating down the river. We paddled out to it, got aboard and climbed in. As we looked in at the window, we saw clothes hanging against the wall, and something lying on the floor in the far corner that looked like a man.

Jim went and looked, and said, "It's a dead man. He's been shot in the back. Come in, Huck, but don't look at his face –it's too ghastly."

I didn't look at the dead man at all. There were lots of clothes hanging against the wall. We put the whole lot into the canoe. The way things were scattered about, we supposed the people left in a hurry. We got an old tin lantern, too.

Then I paddled over to the Illinois shore, and we got back safely to the island. After breakfast I wanted to talk about the dead man and work out how he came to be killed; but Jim didn't want to. He said it would come and haunt us. So I didn't say anything more.

The days went along; life was getting slow and dull. I decided to slip over to the other side of the river and find out what was going on there. Jim liked the idea, but said I must be careful. He told me that I must go in the dark and dress up like a girl.

So, we took one of the calico gowns that we got from the boat. I turned up my trouser-legs to my knees and got into the gown. It was a pretty good fit. I put on a sunbonnet too. Jim looked at me carefully and said nobody would know me now. All the day I practised moving around in these clothes to get the hang of things, and soon I could do pretty well in them. But Jim said I didn't walk like a girl; and he said I must quit pulling up my gown to get at my pant-pocket.

I took note of it, and did better. I started up the Illinois shore in the canoe just after dark and reached at the bottom of the town. I tied up my canoe and walked along the bank. I saw a light burning in a little shanty and I slipped up and peeped in at the window.

There was a woman about forty year old, knitting by a candle. She was a stranger, for I knew every face in that town. Now this was lucky. If this woman had been in such a little town for two days, she could tell me all I wanted to know. So I knocked at the door and decided that I wouldn't forget I was a girl now.

The woman opened the door, called me inside and looked me all over. "What might your name be?" she asked.

"Sarah Williams."

"Where do you live? Here?"

"No, ma'am. In Hookerville, seven miles down the river. I've walked all the way and I'm all tired out."

"Hungry, too, I think. I'll find you something."

"No ma'am, I am not hungry. I was so hungry I had to stop two miles below here at a farm; so I am not hungry any more. It's what makes me so late. My mother's down sick and out of money and everything, and I come to tell my uncle Abner Moore. He lives at the upper end of the town. I haven't ever been here before. Do you know him?"

"No; but I don't know everybody yet. I haven't lived here quite two weeks. It's a considerable ways to the upper end of the considerable ways to the upper end of the town. You better stay here all night. Take off your bonnet."

"No," I said; "I think I'll rest for a while, and go on. I am not afraid of the dark."

However, she wouldn't let me go all that way by myself, but said that soon her husband would be home and she would send him with me. Then the woman started talking about her family and relations and neighbourhood, and so on. She talked for over an hour about her problems. Finally, she got to the news about my murder.

"Who did it?" I asked her.

"Some think old Finn did it himself."

"No—is that so?"

"Almost everybody thought it at first. He'll never know how high he came to getting hanged. But before night, they changed their minds and judged it was done by a runaway slave named Jim."

"Why, he..."

I stopped myself. I reckoned I better keep quiet. The woman kept talking, and never noticed I had said anything at all.

"The slave ran off the very night Huck Finn was killed. So there's a reward of three hundred dollars for him. And there's a reward for old Finn, too—two hundred dollars.

You see, old Finn came to town the morning after the murder, and told about it. He went out on the ferryboat hunt; and right after that he just upped and left. Before night they wanted to hang him, but he was gone, you see. Well, next day they found out the slave was gone, and that he hadn't been seen since ten o'clock the night the murder was done. So they put the blame on him, you see.

Next day, old Finn came back, and went boo-hooing to Judge Thatcher to get money to hunt for the slave. The judge gave him some, and that very evening he got drunk. He was around till late at night with a couple of tough looking strangers, and then went off with them. Well, he hasn't come back since, and people now think that he killed his own boy and fixed things so that folks would think robbers did it. Oh, he's sly, I reckon. If he doesn't come back for a year he'll be all right. You can't prove anything on him, you know; everything will be quietened down then, and he'll walk into Huck's money easily."

"Does everybody think the slave did the murder? I said.

"Oh, no, not everybody. But many people think he did it. But they will get the slave pretty soon, and then they will scare it out of him."

"Why, are they still after him?"

"Does three hundred dollars lay around every day for people to pick up? Some folks think the slave isn't far from here. I'm one of them—but I haven't talked it around. A few days ago I'd seen smoke coming from Jackson's Island.

I know no one lives over there, so maybe the slave is hiding there. When husband returned home about two hours back, I sent him to find it out—him and another man."

I got so uneasy to hear this that I couldn't sit still. I had to do something with my hands; so I took up a needle from the table and started threading it. My hands shook, and I was making a bad job of it.

When the woman stopped talking, I looked up. There she was, looking at me curiously and smiling a little.

I didn't feel a bit comfortable.

Pretty soon she said, "What did you say your name was, honey?"

"M—Mary Williams."

"Honey, I thought you said it was Sarah when you first came in?"

"Oh, yes ma'am, I did. Sarah Mary Williams. Sarah's my first name. Some call me Sarah, some call me Mary."

I was feeling better then, but I wished I was out of there, anyway.

Soon, the woman began telling me how hard times were and how rats roamed as freely in the house as if they owned it. She had to have things handy to throw at them when she was alone, or they wouldn't give her any peace. She showed me a bar of lead twisted up into a knot, and told me to throw it at the mice. I wanted to get away before the old man got back, and threw a good shot. She said that was first rate, and then brought along a hank of yarn which she wanted me to help her with. I held up my two hands and she put the hank over them and again started talking about her and her husband's matters. But, suddenly she stopped chatting and said, "Better keep watching the rats."

She dropped the lead into my lap, and I clapped my legs together on it. Then, after a minute, she took off the hank and looked me straight in the face, and said very pleasantly, "Come, now, what's your real name?"

"Wh—what, mum?"

"What's your real name? Is it Bill, or Tom, or Bob?—or what is it?"

I reckon I shook like a leaf, and I didn't know hardly what to do.

"Sit down. I am not going to hurt you. You just tell me your secret, and trust me. I'll keep it; and, what's more, I'll help you. I see that you've been treated badly, and have made up your mind to run away. Bless you, child, I wouldn't tell on you. Tell me all about it now, that's a good boy."

I decided it wouldn't be any use to pretend any longer. So I told her my father and mother were dead, and the law had bound me out to a mean old farmer, who treated me so bad I couldn't stand it any longer. He went away for a couple of days, and so I stole some of his daughter's old clothes and ran away. I said I

believed my uncle Abner Moore would take care of me, and so that was why I struck out for this town of Goshen.

"Goshen, child? This isn't Goshen. This is St. Petersburg. Goshen's ten mile further up the river."

"Well, it doesn't matter now. I got to be moving along. I'll reach Goshen before daylight."

"Wait a minute. I'll put you up a snack to eat. You might want it." So she put me up a snack, and said, "Now answer truly; what's your real name?"

"George Peters, mum."

"Well, try to remember it, George. Don't forget and tell me it's Alexander before you go, and then get out by saying its George Alexander when I catch you. And although you might fool men, don't go near women wearing that old gown.

And, when you are to thread a needle, don't hold the thread still and bring the needle up to it. But, hold the needle still and poke the thread at it; that's the way a woman always does, but a man always does the other way.

And when you throw at a rat or anything, hold yourself on tiptoe and fetch your hand up over your head as awkwardly as you can, and miss your rat, like a girl will do. And, mind you, when a girl tries to catch anything in her lap she throws her knees apart; she doesn't clap them together, the way you did when you caught the lump of lead. Why, I knew you were a boy when you were threading the needle! I planned the other things just to make sure.

Now trot along to your uncle, Sarah Mary Williams George Alexander Peters, and if you get into trouble you send word to Mrs. Judith Loftus, which is me, and I'll do what I can to get you out of it."

I got out of the house and made straight for my canoe. I rowed with all my might trying to get to the island as fast as I could. As soon as I

reached Jackson's island, I ran towards Jim and said, "Get up Jim! There isn't a minute to lose. They're after us!"

Jim never asked any questions, but the way he worked for the next half an hour showed just how much he was scared. We had all the things back in our raft. We put out the campfire at the cavern. I took the canoe out from the shore and tied it onto the raft. Then we slipped along down the river, past the foot of the island never saying a word.

CHAPTER 5

Living under the Star-lit Sky

When the first streak of day began to show, we tied up in a big bend on the Illinois side, hacked off cottonwood branches, and covered up the raft with them. Then, when it was dark, we pulled out the raft and drifted down the river.

We passed towns that looked like shiny beds of lights; not a house could be seen on its own. Each night at about ten o'clock, I used to slip ashore at some little village and buy ten or fifteen cents' worth of meal or bacon or other stuff to eat. And everyday, before daylight, I slipped into cornfields and borrowed a watermelon, or a mushmelon, or a pumpkin, or some new corn. Pap always said there wasn't any harm in borrowing things if you meant to pay them back some time. But the widow said that taking things from others wasn't anything but a soft name for stealing. Jim reckoned the widow was partly right and Pap was partly right. So we talked it over and decided to drop half the things from the list – we won't borrow these any more. But there won't be any harm in borrowing the other half, we decided.

On the fifth night, a big storm rose after midnight, with tremendous thunder and lightning, and the rain poured down in a solid sheet. We stayed inside the tent we had built on the raft.

Once, when the lightning flashed I could see a steamboat on the river. She was leaning over, with part of her upper deck above water. I wanted to get aboard of her and sneak around a little, and see what was there. But Jim was dead against it at first.

"Do you reckon Tom Sawyer would ever go by this thing?" I said. "He'd call it an adventure – and he'd land on that wreck. And wouldn't he throw style into it? I wish Tom Sawyer WAS here."

Jim grumbled a little, but gave in. We went sneaking down the slope of the boat towards the deck. Then we climbed to the front of the captain's door, which was open, and saw a light! And, at the same moment, we heard low voices.

Jim whispered to me that he was feeling very sick, and told me to come along. So, both of us were going to start for the raft; but just then I heard a voice cry out, "Oh, please don't, boys; I swear I won't ever tell!"

Another voice said, pretty loud, "It's a lie, Jim Turner. You've acted this way before. You've always wanted more than your share of the loot, and you've got it too. But this time, you've told just one time too many. You're the meanest, treacherousest hound in this country."

I turned towards Jim, but by this time he had left for the raft. But I had got pretty curious now. I said to myself, Tom Sawyer wouldn't back out now, and so I won't either; I'm going to see what's going on here. So I dropped on my hands and knees in the little passage, crept along till I came to a room, and peeped inside.

There were three men in the room, two of whom tied up the third one. It became quite clear to me that they were robbers. One of the robbers wanted to kill the prisoner immediately, but the other man held him back. Finally, the two men decided to leave their partner on the boat and wait until it sank.

"He'll be drowned, and won't have anybody

to blame for it but his own self. I reckon that's a greatly better than killing him," said the man called Packard.

"But suppose the boat DON'T break up and wash off?" asked his partner.

"Well, we can wait the two hours anyway and see, can't we?"

"All right, then; come along."

So, both of them started.

I scrambled forward in a cold sweat towards the raft. It was dark as pitch and I stumbled over something. It was Jim.

I said, "Quick, Jim, there's no time; there's a gang of murderers over there, and if we don't find their boat and set it drifting down the river, these fellows would get away and their partner would be in a bad fix. But if we do find their boat, we can put ALL of them in a bad fix! Quick, you start the raft, and..."

"Oh, my lord, lord! RAFF'? Here isn't no raff'!" screamed Jim. "She broke loose and gone!

And here we is!!"

I caught my breath and almost fainted. Shut up on a wreck, and with such a bunch of criminals as that! But it wasn't any time to be sentimentering. We just GOT to find that boat now, and have it for ourselves.

So, quaking and shaking we went towards the stern, to search for the boat. And when we got pretty close to the cross-hall door, sure enough, there was the boat! We sure were glad!

But just then the door opened. One of the men stuck his head out, flung a bag of something into the boat, and then got inside. It was Packard. Then his mate, Bill came out and got in.

"All ready—shove off the boat!" said Packard, in a low voice.

Hearing this, I felt so weak I could hardly stand still. Then Bill said, "Hold on—did you check him?"

"No. Didn't you?"

"No. So he's still got his share of the money."

"Well, then, come along; we can't leave money."

The two went inside the cabin, and the door slammed shut. In a half second, I was inside the boat and Jim came tumbling after me. I cut the rope with my knife, and away we went! We went gliding swiftly along, dead silent, then in a second or two more we were a hundred yards away from the wreck.

We were safe!

When we were three or four hundred yards downstream, we saw a little spark on deck. It was the robber's lantern.

Clearly, the robbers had found out that their boat was gone, and that now they were in as much trouble as their prisoner, Jim Turner.

Then Jim manned the oars, and we began to look out for our raft. Now for the first time I began to worry about the men. I began to think how dreadful it was, even for murderers, to be in such a fix. So I said to Jim, "The first light we see, we'll land, and find a place where it's a good hiding-place for you and the boat."

Pretty soon it began to storm again. This time, it was worse than ever. The rain poured down. We boomed along down the river, watching for lights and looking for our raft. By and by, it stopped raining, but the clouds remained.

Then a flash showed us the raft floating, and we rowed towards it.

We were sure glad to get aboard the raft again. The boat was half full of plunder which that gang had stolen from the steamboat. We piled the loot on to the raft. Then I told Jim to float along down the river, and show a light when he figured he had gone about two miles. He was to keep it burning until I came.

Meanwhile, I manned my oars and rowed towards the light. As I got down towards it, three or four more lights showed up. It was a village. As I went floating by in my boat towards the shore light, I saw it was a lantern hanging on the jack-staff of a ferryboat. I looked around for the watchman; and by and by I found him dozing, with his head down between his knees. I gave the watchman's shoulder two or three little shoves, and began to cry.

He stirred up.

I made up a story as to how my family crashed into the wreck while travelling down the river, and that they were stuck there. I was the only one who could swim, and so I had come to get help. The old man immediately got his ferry moving. However, before he had gone very far, the wreck floated by. It was sinking even further down the river. I realized that there wasn't much chance for anybody being alive in her. I felt a little bit heavy-hearted about the gang.

It did seem a powerful long time before Jim's light showed up; and when it did show it looked like it was a thousand miles off. By the time I got there, the sky was beginning to get a little grey in the east. We tied the boat to the raft and struck for an island. Once we reached it, we hid the raft, sunk the boat, turned in and slept like dead people.

By and by, when we got up, we turned over the robbers' plunder and found boots, and blankets, clothes, and a lot of books, a spyglass, and three boxes of cigars. We hadn't ever been this rich before in either of our lives!

We kept sailing down the river for some more days.

We reckoned that some more nights would take us to Cairo. There, we would sell the raft, get on a steamboat and go way up the Ohio amongst the free States where slavery is banned, and then be out of trouble forever.

Two or three days and nights went by. I might say they slid along in a quiet and smooth sort of way. At some distance were the banks and the islands, across the water; and maybe a spark—which was a candle in a cabin window; and sometimes you could hear a fiddle or a song coming over from one of them.

It was lovely to live on a raft. When we lay down at night, we saw the sky up there all speckled with stars, and we used to discuss whether they were made or only just happened. Jim thought that they were made, but I believed that they just happened.

Once or twice we would see a steamboat slipping along in the dark. Now and then it would belch out a whole world of sparks out of its chimneys, and the sparks would rain down on the river, and look awfully pretty; and then she would turn a corner and her lights would wink out. After midnight the people on shore went to bed, and then for two or three hours the shore was black—no more sparks in the cabin windows. The sparks worked as our clock— the first one that showed again meant morning was coming.

CHAPTER 6

The Duke and the King

One morning around daybreak, I paddled up a stream amongst the cypress woods, to see if I could get some berries.

Just as I was passing by a kind of cow-path, a couple of men came running up the path towards me. Whenever I saw anybody running, I thought it was for ME—or maybe Jim. So, I was about to run away from there quickly, when they called out to me and begged me to save their lives. They said that they were being chased by men and dogs.

I felt sorry for them and asked them to jump into my raft. They did so, and as soon as they were aboard, I made for our towhead. In about five or ten minutes we heard the dogs and the men away off, shouting.

One of these fellows was of about seventy years of age, or more, and had a bald head and very grey whiskers. He wore an old battered-up hat, a greasy blue woollen shirt, ragged old blue jeans breeches stuffed into his boot-tops, and home-knit galoshes. He had an old long-tailed blue jeans coat with slick brass buttons flung over his arm, and both of them had big, fat, ratty-looking carpet-bags. The other fellow was about thirty, and dressed nearly as ordinarily.

After breakfast we all rested down and talked. The first thing that came out was that these chaps didn't know one another. The bald headed man told us that he had been selling medicines that were meant to take the tartar off people's teeth. The trouble was that the medicine took off the enamel as well!

The younger man had been holding temperance meetings where he lectured people about the evils of drinking. He had been making up to ten dollars a night. But then one night he was caught drinking himself, and so he had to run for his life.

Then the two of them got talking and decided that they should team up in business and travel together. Suddenly, in the middle of the talking, the younger man heaved a sigh and cried, "Alas!"

"What are you alas' ing about?" said the bald headed man. "My poor heart is broken," cried the younger man, "for I have fallen so low from so high a position." And he began to wipe the corner of his eye with a rag.

Then he said, very solemnly, "Gentlemen, I

will reveal the secret of my birth to you, for I feel I may have confidence in you. By rights I am the Duke of Bridgewater!"

He went on to tell us how his great grandfather's brother seized the nobleman's title after his death, even though they should rightfully have been passed onto his grandfather, father, and then him.

The story moved both Jim and me and we tried to console him. All through dinner we stood around and waited on him.

After a while, the other man – the bald-headed one, got pretty quiet. He didn't seem to like all the special treatment the duke was getting.

"Looky here, Bilgewater," he said, "I am sorry for you, but you aren't the only person with these troubles. I too have a secret. I am actually the King, or Louis the Seventeenth, the son of Louis the Sixteenth and Marry Antoinette."

"You! At your age! No! You must be six or

seven hundred years old, at the very least," said the duke.

"Trouble has done it, Bilgewater, trouble has done it; trouble bring in these grey hairs and this premature baldness.

Yes, gentlemen, you see before you, in blue jeans and misery, the wandering, exiled and suffering rightful King of France."

It didn't take me long to make up my mind that these liars weren't any kings nor dukes at all, but just low-down humbugs and frauds. But I never said anything, because I didn't want to get into any trouble. If they wanted us to call themselves kings and dukes, I didn't have any objections. The best way to get along with this kind of people was to let them have their own way.

However, it was of no use to tell Jim about it, so I didn't tell him.

The two asked us many questions; they wanted to know why did we cover up the raft

at daytime, and lay by in the daytime instead of rowing on? Was Jim a runaway slave?

"Goodness sakes!" said I. "Would a runaway slave run SOUTH?"

No, they agreed, he wouldn't.

I had to explain things some way, so I told them that I was a farmer's son. My pap and my brother had died. Jim was the last slave our family owned. I was travelling south to Orleans to live with Uncle Ben. We travelled at night because people who thought Jim was a runaway slave kept harassing us.

We dared not stop at any town for days and days; kept right along down the river. We were down south in the warm weather now, and a long, long way from home. We began to come to trees with Spanish moss on them. It was the first I ever saw growing, and it made the woods look solemn and dismal.

CHAPTER 7

The Royal Nonesuch

One morning, the king and the duke came out of the tent looking quite rusty. But after they jumped overboard and took a swim, it cheered them up a good deal. After breakfast, the king took a seat on the corner of the raft. Then he pulled off his boots, rolled up his breeches, let his legs dangle in the water, lit his pipe, and went to getting his Romeo and Juliet by heart. Then, he and the duke began to practice it together.

Next, they got out a couple of long swords that the duke made out of oak wood and began to practice sword fight.

The duke called himself Richard III; and the way they pranced around the raft was grand to see. But, by and by the king tripped and fell overboard. After that, they took a rest, and had a talk about all kinds of adventures they'd had in other times along the river.

Soon, the two frauds decided that the first town we reached, they would hire a hall and put on a play. At the first chance he got, the duke had some show-bills printed. After that, all the time for two or three days, there wasn't anything but sword fighting going on the raft.

One morning, we came to a little town about three miles down a big bend. So we tied up about three-quarters of a mile above the bend, in the mouth of a crick which was shut in like a tunnel by the cypress trees. All of us except Jim boarded the canoe and went down to the town to see if there was any chance in that place for our show.

We got to know that there was going to be a circus there that afternoon and we thought that was quite lucky for us.

The country people were already beginning to come in, in all kinds of old wagons, and on horses. The circus would leave before night, so our show would have a pretty good chance. The duke hired the courthouse, and we went around and stuck up the bills. The bills read like this:

SHAKSPEREAN REVIVAL!
WONDERFUL ATTRACTION!
FOR ONE NIGHT ONLY!
THE WORLD RENOWNED
TRAGEDIANS,
DAVID GARRICK THE YOUNGER,
AND

EDMUND KEAN THE ELDER,
IN THEIR SUBLIME SHAKSPEREAN
SPECTACLE ENTITLED
THE BALCONY SCENE
IN
ROMEO AND JULIET!
ROMEO..................MR. GARRICK
JULIET.................MR. KEAN
Also:
THE THRILLING, MASTERLY, AND BLOOD-CURDLING BROAD-SWORD CONFLICT
IN RICHARD III!
RICHARD III............MR. GARRICK
RICHMOND...............MR. KEAN
Admission 25 cents.

I went to the circus and lingered around the backside till the watchman went away for a while; and then I dived in under the tent. Though I had my twenty-dollar gold piece and some other money, but I reckoned I better save it, because one never knew how soon you are going to need it, away from home and amongst strangers.

The circus was pretty splendid. The men and women went leaping and dancing through the air. The ladies looked just like queens, dressed in clothes that cost millions of dollars, and just littered with diamonds. I never saw anything so lovely. All through the circus they did the most astonishing things; and all the time the clown made the people die laughing.

That night, we had OUR show. But, only about twelve people had come to see it - just enough to pay off our expenses. Besides, the people laughed all the time, and that made the duke really mad. Anyway, everybody left before the show was over; everybody, except one boy.

He was asleep.

The duke said these silly villagers couldn't understand Shakespeare; what they wanted was low comedy. So, next morning he got some big sheets of wrapping paper and some black paint, and drew off some handbills, and stuck them up all over the village.

The bills said:

AT THE COURT HOUSE!
FOR 3 NIGHTS ONLY!
THE WORLD-RENOWNED TRAGEDIANS
DAVID GARRICK THE YOUNGER!
AND
EDMUND KEAN THE ELDER!
IN THEIR THRILLING TRAGEDY OF
THE KING'S CAMELEOPARD,
OR
THE ROYAL NONESUCH!
Admission 50 cents.

Then at the bottom was the biggest line of all, which said:

LADIES AND CHILDREN
NOT ADMITTED.

The entire day the king worked hard, rigging up a stage and a curtain and a row of candles for footlights.

That night the house was jam full of men. When the place couldn't hold any more, the duke quit tending the door.

He came on to the stage, stood up before the curtain and made a little speech. He praised up this tragedy, and said it was the most thrilling one that ever was. He went on bragging about the tragedy, and about Edmund Kean the Elder, who was to play the main part in it.

At last, when he'd got everybody's expectations up high enough, he rolled up the curtain. And the next minute, the king came prancing out on all fours, naked!

He was painted all over, with stripes of all sorts of colours, as splendid as a rainbow.

And… but never mind the rest of his outfit; it was just wild, but it was awful funny. The people almost killed themselves laughing; and when the king had finished capering, and went off behind the scenes, they roared and clapped and stormed and haw hawed till he came back and did it over again, and after that they made him do it yet another time.

Then, the duke let the curtain down, bowed to the people, and said the great tragedy will be performed only two nights more. And then he made them another bow, and said if he had succeeded in pleasing them, he will be deeply obliged if they would go and tell their friends about it, so that they too might come and see the wonderful show for themselves.

Twenty people sang out, "What, is it over? Is that ALL?"

The duke said yes, it was. Then there was a fine hullabaloo. Everybody shouted, "Cheat!" and were about to rush towards the stage for the tragedians. But then, a big, fine looking man jumped up on a bench and shouted, "Hold on, just a word, gentlemen!"

The people stopped to listen.

"We are cheated – badly cheated. But we don't want to be the laughing stock of this whole town. If we let this out, we will never hear the last of this thing as long as we live. No, what we want is to go out of here quietly, and talk this show up, and trick the REST of the town! Then we'll all be in the same boat. Isn't that sensible?"

"You bet it is! ... The judge is right!" everybody sang out.

"All right, then, not a word about any cheating. Go home, and advise everybody to come and see the tragedy."

Next day, you couldn't hear anything around that town but how splendid that show was. The house was jammed again that night, and the king and duke cheated this crowd the same way as before.

When we got home to the raft after the show, we all had a supper. By and by, around midnight, they made Jim and me back out the raft and float her down the middle of the river. Then we were to fetch her in and hide her about two miles below town.

The third night the house was crammed again. But this time there weren't any newcomers, but people who were at the show the other two nights. I stood near the duke at the door, and I saw that every man that went in had his pockets bulging, or something muffled up under his coat. I smelt rotten eggs, and rotten cabbages, and such things.

The smell was so strong that I couldn't stand it and had to move away. And when the place couldn't hold any more people, the duke gave a fellow a coin and told him to tend the door for him a minute. Then he started around for the stage door, and I went after him. But the minute we turned the corner, he said, "Now walk fast, till you get away from the houses. And then run for the raft as fast as you can!"

I did so, and he did the same. We reached the raft at the same time, and in less than two seconds we were gliding down stream, and edging towards the middle of the river. Nobody said a word.

I had thought that the poor king was in for some terrible time with the audience. But it was nothing of the sort.

Pretty soon, he crawled out from under the tent, and said, "Well, how did the plan work this time, duke?"

The king hadn't gone to the town at all!

We rowed in darkness till we were about ten miles below the village. Then we lit up and had a supper. The king and the duke nearly laughed off their heads over the way they had fooled the people. The duke said, "Sillies, dumbheads!

I knew the first house would keep mum and would let the rest of the town get roped in. I knew too that they would lie waiting for us the third night, and consider it was THEIR turn now. Well, it IS their turn, and I'd give something to know how they are doing now. They can turn the show into a picnic if they like – they brought plenty rotten eggs and vegetables!"

The tricksters had taken in four hundred and sixty-five dollars in three nights. I had never seen money hauled in by the wagon-load like that before.

By and by, when they were asleep and snoring, Jim said, "Don't it surprise you the way the king carries on, Huck?"

"No," I said, "it doesn't."

"Why don't it, Huck?"

"Well, it doesn't because it's in the breed. I reckon they're all alike," said I.

"But, Huck, these kings of ours are regular rogues. That's just what they are; regular rogues!" Jim exclaimed.

"Well, that's what I'm saying; all kings are mostly rogues, as far as I can make out."

What was the use to tell Jim these weren't real kings and dukes? It wouldn't have done any good; and, besides, it was just as I said: you

couldn't tell them from the real sort.

I went to sleep, and Jim didn't call me when it was my turn to watch. He often did that. When I woke up just at daybreak, Jim was sitting there with his head down between his knees, moaning and mourning to himself. I knew what it was about. He was thinking about his wife and his children back home, and was low and homesick. I do believe Jim cared just as much for his people, as white folks did for theirs.

Often at nights, when he thought I was asleep, he kept grieving away and saying, "Poor little Elizabeth! Poor little Johnny! It's mighty hard to think I am going to see you no more, no more!"

Jim was a real good fellow.

CHAPTER 8

The Disgraceful Scheme

The next night, we laid up under a little willow growing in the middle of the river. There was a village on each side of the river. The duke and the king began to lay out a plan for working them. These rogues wanted to try the Nonesuch again, because there was so much money in it. But they judged it wouldn't be safe, because maybe the news might have worked along down by this time. The king announced that he would drop over to the other village without any plan, and just trust in Providence to show him a profitable way.

We had all bought store clothes at our last stop; and now the king put his on, and he told me to put mine on. I did it, of course. The king's duds were all black, and he did look real swell and solemn. I never before knew how much clothes could change a person's look; so grand and good and pious did the king look!

Jim cleaned up the canoe, and I got my paddle ready. There was a big steamboat laying at the shore, about three mile above the town – it had been there a couple of hours, taking on freight.

Said the king, "Seeing how I'm dressed, it would be better to say that I arrived down from St. Louis or Cincinnati, or some other big place. Go for the steamboat, Huckleberry; we'll go down to the village on her."

I didn't have to be ordered twice to go and take a steamboat ride.

I paddled up river close to the shore, and pretty soon, we come to a nice innocent-looking young country boy sitting on a log, swabbing the sweat off his face. The weather was quite warm; and he had a couple of big carpetbags near him.

"Turn the canoe in shore," the king told me.

I did so.

"Where are you bound for, young man?" the king called out to the boy.

"For the steamboat; going to Orleans," the boy replied.

"Get aboard," said the king. "Hold on a minute, my servant will help you with the bags. Jump out and help the gentleman, Adolphus."

The crook, he meant ME to be his servant!

However, I did so, and then the three of us started on again. The young chap was very thankful and said it was tough work tugging along his baggage in such weather. He asked the king where he was going, and the king told him he'd come down the river to see an old friend on a farm up the river.

The young fellow said, "When I first saw you I thought, 'It's Mr. Wilks, surely, and he has very nearly arrived on time.' You aren't him, are you?" The king said, "No, my name's REVEREND Alexander Blodgett. But still I'm sorry for Mr. Wilks for not arriving in time; I hope he hasn't missed anything."

"Well, he didn't miss any property by it, because he'll get that all right; but he's missed seeing his brother Peter die.

His brother talked about nothing but him all these three weeks; he hadn't seen him since they were boys together – and hadn't ever seen his brother William at all – that's the deaf and dumb one. Peter and George were the only ones that come out here. George was the married brother; he and his wife both died last

year. Harvey and William are the only ones that are left now."

"Did anybody send them word?" asked the king.

"Oh, yes; a month or two ago, when Peter first fell sick, because Peter said that he felt like he wasn't going to get well this time. You see, as he was pretty old, and George's girls were too young to be much company for him, except for Mary Jane, so he was kind of lonesome after George and his wife died, and didn't seem to care much to live. He most desperately wanted to see Harvey and William. He left a letter behind for Harvey, and said he'd written in it where his money was hid, and how he wanted the rest of the property divided up so George's girls would be all right – for George didn't leave back anything."

"Where does Harvey live?" said the king.

"Oh, he lives in England – Sheffield – preaches there – hasn't ever been in this country."

"Too bad he couldn't have lived to see his brothers, poor soul," said the king. "You are going to Orleans, you said?" said the king.

"Yes, and I'm going in a ship, next Wednesday, for Rio Janeiro, where my uncle lives."

"It's a pretty long journey. But it'll be lovely; wish I was going too. Is Mary Jane the oldest? How old are the others?" said the king.

"Mary Jane's nineteen, Susan's fifteen, and Joanna is about fourteen."

"Poor things! To be left alone in the cold world so."

Well, the old man went on asking questions till he quite emptied that young fellow. He inquired about everybody and everything in that town and all about the Wilks, and so on.

Then he asked, "Was Peter Wilks well off?"

"Oh, yes, pretty well off. He had houses and land, and it's reckoned he left three or four thousand in cash hidden up somewhere."

"When did you say he died?"

"I didn't say, but it was last night."

"Well, it's all terribly sad; but we've all got to go, one time or another. So we should be prepared."

"Yes, sir, it's the best way. Ma used to always say that."

When we reached the steamboat she had almost finished loading, and pretty soon she got off. The king never said anything about going aboard, so I lost my ride, after all. When the boat was gone the king made me paddle up another mile to a lonesome place, and then he got ashore and said, "Now quickly go back and fetch the duke up here, and the new carpet-bags as well."

I saw what HE was up to; but of course I didn't say anything. When I got back with the duke, we hid the canoe.

Then they sat down on a log, and the king told him everything the young fellow had said, and added, "How are you at playing deaf and dumb, Bilgewater?"

The duke told him to leave it to him; as he had played the role of deaf and dumb in dramas.

About the middle of the afternoon we saw a big boat and got aboard her. When they found we wanted to go only four or five miles, the captain became pretty angry and said he wouldn't land us. But the king was calm and offered the captain a few extra dollars. This softened him down and he said it was all right. When we got to the village, about two dozen men flocked down on seeing the steamboat.

Then the king said, "Can any of you gentlemen tell me where Mr. Peter Wilks lives?"

The men glanced at one another, and nodded their heads, as much as to say, "What did I tell you?" Then one of them said in a soft and gentle kind of way, "I'm sorry, sir; but he no more."

All of a sudden, the sly old king fell against the man, put his chin on the man's shoulder, and cried down his back.

"Alas, alas, our poor brother – gone, and we never got to see him; oh, it's too, too hard!"

Then he turned around, blubbering, and made a lot of idiotic signs with his hands to the duke. The duke immediately dropped a carpet-bag and burst out crying too. The men gathered around and sympathized with them, and said all sorts of kind things to them, and carried their carpet-bags up the hill for them, while the two cried and lamented like they had lost everything in the world.

If these two weren't the meanest lot that ever I saw! It was enough to make a person ashamed of the human race.

CHAPTER 9

I Goof Up

The news was all over town in two minutes, and the people came tearing down. Pretty soon we were in the middle of a crowd. The windows and dooryards were full; and every minute somebody would say, over a fence, "Is it THEM?"

When we got to the house the three girls were standing in the door. Mary Jane was awfully beautiful, and her face and her eyes were all lit up, she was so glad her uncles had come. The king spread his arms and Mary Jane rushed towards him and hugged him, and the other two girls hugged the duke.

Everybody around started crying for joy to see them meet again at last!

Then the king and the duke, with a hand across each other's shoulder, and the other hand to their eyes, walked slowly and solemnly towards the coffin that was placed in a corner. All the talking stopped and people said, "Sh!"

Men took off their hats and drooped their heads, so that one could a heard a pin fall.

And when they got there and looked into the coffin, the two burst out crying so loudly you could have heard them up to Orleans! Then they put their arms around each other's necks, hung their chins over each other's shoulders; and then for three or four minutes, I never saw two men cry the way they did. And then all the people around too started crying like anything.

I never saw anything so disgusting!

Well, by and by the king got up and made a speech about it being a sore trial for him and his poor brother to lose the diseased (deceased). Then he said how he and his nieces would be glad if a few of the principal friends of the family would take supper here with them this evening.

The king babbled along and managed to inquire about pretty much everybody in town by his name, including dogs, and mentioned all sorts of little things that happened one time or another in the town. And he always said that Peter wrote him the things. But that was a lie: he got every one of them out of that young boy in the boat.

Then Mary Jane fetched the letter her father left behind. The king read it out and cried over it. It gave the house and three thousand dollars in gold to the girls; and some other houses and land worth about seven thousand, and three thousand dollars in gold to Harvey and William. It also told where the six thousand cash was hidden down in the cellar.

So these two frauds said they'd go and bring it up and have everything open and correct. They told me to come along with a candle. We shut the cellar door behind us, and when they found the bag they spilt it out on the floor. It was a lovely sight – all the gold coins. My, the way the king's eyes did shine!

The two pawed the coins, sifted them through their fingers and let them jingle down on the floor.

Almost everybody would have been satisfied with the pile; but no, these two had to count it.

So they counted it, and it came out four hundred and fifteen dollars short of the six thousand.

They worried over that for a while and ransacked all around for the remaining money.

"Hold on," the duke said, suddenly; "let's make up the deficit," and he begun to haul out gold coins out of his pocket.

"It's a dreadfully good idea, duke," said the king. "The old Nonesuch helped us out again!"

It almost made them penniless, but they made up the six thousand.

"I got another idea," said the duke, "Let's go upstairs and count this money, and then GIVE IT TO THE GIRLS."

"Let me hug you! It's the most dazzling idea!! This will take care of any of their suspicions," said the king.

When we got upstairs everybody gathered around the table. The king counted the coins, stacked it up, and then put it back into the bag again. Next, I saw the king begin to swell himself up for another speech. He said, "Friends, my poor brother has done generously for them that are left behind in the vale of sorrows. He has done generously for these poor little lambs that he loved and sheltered, and that's left fatherless and motherless. Here, Mary Jane, Susan, Joanna, take the money – take it ALL."

Mary Jane hugged him. Everybody had tears in their eyes, and almost shook the hands off the frauds, saying all the time, "You dear good souls! How lovely! How COULD you!"

By and by, a big iron-jawed man came in. He stood listening and looking, and not saying anything. Meanwhile, the king went on and on, blabbing in his forged English accent, "...tomorrow we want ALL to come – everybody; for my brother liked everybody, and so it's fitting that his funeral ORGIES should be public."

Suddenly, the iron jawed man laughed right in the king's face. Everybody was shocked. One man said, "Why, Doctor! Haven't you heard the news? This is Harvey Wilks."

"Peter Wilks' brother, indeed!" said the doctor. "It's the worst imitation I ever heard,

He's a fraud, that's what he is!"

All were shocked! They crowded around the doctor and tried to quieten him, and tried to explain to him how Harvey had shown in forty ways that he WAS Harvey, and knew everybody by name, and the names of the dogs as well.

All of a sudden, the doctor turned to the three girls and said, "I was your father's friend, and I warn you as a friend that wants to protect you and keep you out of harm, to have nothing to do with these frauds. They have come here with a lot of empty names and facts picked up from somewhere, and you take them for PROOFS! Now listen to me; turn these impostors out. Will you?"

Mary Jane straightened herself up, and said, "HERE is my answer."

She lifted up the bag of money and put it in the king's hands, saying, "Take these six thousand dollars, and invest for me and my sisters any way you want to, and don't give us any receipt for it."

Everybody clapped their hands, while the king held up his head and smiled proudly.

The doctor said, "All right; I wash MY hands of the matter. But I warn you all that a time's coming when you're going to feel sick whenever you think of this day."

And he went away.

"All right, doctor," said the king, mocking him; "we'll try and get them to send for you."

WELL, when they were all gone the king asked Mary Jane if they had spare rooms. She said she had one spare room, which would do for Uncle William, and she'd give her own room to Uncle Harvey. Up in the loft was a little place with a straw bed in it and the king said that it would do very well for his servant – meaning me.

That night, they had a big supper, and many men and women were there, and I stood behind the king and the duke's chairs and waited on them, and the slaves waited on the rest. And when it was over, me and Joanna had supper in the kitchen, while the others were helping the slaves clean up the things. Joanna started asking me all sorts of things about England. She said, "Did you ever see the king?"

"Who? William Fourth? Well, I bet I have - he goes to our church."

I knew he was dead years ago, but I never let that on. So when I said he goes to our church, she said, "I thought he lived in London?"

"Well, he does. Where WOULD he live?"

"But I thought YOU lived in Sheffield?"

I saw I was in a mess. I pretended to get choked with a chicken bone, so as to get time to think.

Then I said, "I mean he goes to our church when he's in Sheffield when he comes there to take the sea baths."

"Why, Sheffield isn't on the sea."

"Well, who said it was?"

"Why, you did."

"I DIDN'T, neither."

"You did!"

At this moment Mary Jane stepped in with Susan behind her.

"Joe, it isn't right for you to talk so to him; he is a stranger and so far from his people," she said. "How would you like to be treated so?"

"I haven't done anything to him. He's told some lies, I reckon, and I said I wouldn't swallow it all."

"He's here in our house and a stranger, and it wasn't good of you to say it. If you were in his place it would make you feel ashamed; and so you oughtn't to say a thing to another person that will make THEM feel ashamed."

"Why, he said –"

"It doesn't make any difference what he SAID. The thing is for you to treat him KIND, and not say things to make him remember he isn't amongst his own folks. Ask his pardon." Joanna did so. And did so beautifully!

And I thought, I'm LETTING that old reptile rob these GOOD and KIND girls of their money!

I felt so mean and low down, that I made up my mind: I'll have that money for them or bust! When I was alone, I got the chance to think things over. Shall I go and tell Mary Jane? No, her face would give them a hint, and they'd get away with the money. If she was to obtain help, I'd get mixed up in the business before it was over. No; there was only one way out. I got to steal that money, somehow; and hide it; and by and by, when I'm away down the river, I'll write a letter and tell Mary Jane where it's hid.

I decided to search the rooms. I recollected the king wouldn't let anybody else take care of that money but his own self; and so I went to his room and began to look around there. All of a sudden, I heard the sound of footsteps. I jumped in behind the curtains and snuggled in amongst the gowns, and stood there perfectly still.

The king and duke came in and shut the door. After they sat down, the king said, "Well, what is it?"

"That doctor lays on my mind," said the duke. "We better run out of this, down the river with what we've got."

The king broke out and said, "What! And not sell out the rest of the property? Leave eight or nine thousand dollars' worth of property just lying around?"

The duke grumbled and said the bag of gold was enough, but, at last he gave in, and said all right.

So they got ready to go down stairs again.

As soon as they were gone, I quickly got out of my hiding place, and soon found out the bag of gold that was hidden under the bed. Next I tiptoed along, and got down stairs. The door

was open into the parlour, where the coffin was lying. Just then I heard somebody coming down the stairs, back behind me. I ran in the parlour and swiftly looked around. As the only hiding place I could see was in the coffin, I tucked the moneybag in under its lid just near where Peter Wilks' hands were crossed. They were so cold it made me creep, and I ran back across the room and in behind the door.

The person coming was Mary Jane. She went to the coffin, kneeled down and looked in; then she put up her handkerchief and began to cry. As her back was to me, I slid out, and slipped up to bed, feeling rather depressed.

For now the thing that was going to happen was, the money would be found when they came to screw on the lid.

Then the king would get it again, and it would be a long while before he gave anybody another chance to snatch it from him.

I did not know what to do.

CHAPTER 10

The Decision

The next day, however, the undertaker sealed the coffin without looking inside. The funeral took place and the money got buried along with the coffin!

The following morning, as I was coming down the ladder, I came to the girls' room. The door was open, and I saw Mary Jane sitting by her old hair trunk, which was open and she'd been packing things in it – getting ready to go to England. But she had stopped now with a folded gown in her lap, and had her face in her hands, crying.

I felt awful bad to see it; of course anybody would. I went in there and said, "Miss Mary Jane, you can't bear to see people in trouble; and I can't too – almost always. Tell me about it."

So she did. It was about the slaves – I had expected it.

You see, it was like this: saying that he would take the Wilks girls to England, the rogue king had, just the previous day, sold off their estate and the household slaves. He had sent a slave mother to New Orleans and her two sons to Memphis. The scene at the grief-stricken family's separation was quite heart-rending. The Wilks girls too were very upset. It had taken away whatever joy Mary Jane had felt about her England trip.

"Oh, dear, dear, to think they aren't EVER

for you on a piece of paper, and you can read it along the road to Mr. Lothrop's, if you want to. Do you reckon that'll do?"

"Oh, yes."

So I wrote, "I put it in the coffin. It was in there when you were crying there, away in the night. I was behind the door, and I was mighty sorry for you, Miss Mary Jane."

Then she shook me by the hand, hard, and said, "GOOD-bye. I'm going to do everything just as you've told me; and if I don't ever see you again, I shan't ever forget you. And I'll think of you many, many a times, and I'll PRAY for you, too!"

And she was gone.

Towards the end of the afternoon, the two rogues were having a public auction of the Wilks' property. By and by everything was sold – everything but a little old trifling lot in the graveyard. It was like the king wanted to swallow EVERYTHING.

going to see each other any more!" she cried.

It was then I thought I could hide the truth no more. I just had to tell the poor girl.

Then I said, "If you don't mind it, I'll shut the door and bolt it."

After doing so, I came back and sat down again, and said, "I got to tell the truth, and you have to brace up, Miss Mary, because it's a bad kind, and hard to take, but there isn't any help for it. These uncles of yours aren't any uncles at all! They're a couple of frauds."

It jolted her up like anything, of course; but I went right along and told her everything, from where we first met that young boy going up to the steamboat, right through to where she hugged the king at the front door. Mary Jane's face was afire, like sunset.

"Well," I said, "it's a rough gang, these two frauds, and I'm fixed so I got to travel with them a while longer, whether I want to or not – I'd rather not tell you why. There is another person

going to see each other any more!" she cried.

It was then I thought I could hide the truth no more. I just had to tell the poor girl.

Then I said, "If you don't mind it, I'll shut the door and bolt it."

After doing so, I came back and sat down again, and said, "i got to tell the truth, and you have to brace up, Miss Mary, because it's a bad kind, and hard to take, but there isn't any help for it. These uncles of yours aren't any uncles at all! They're a couple of frauds."

It jolted her up like anything, of course; but I went right along and told her everything, from where we first met that young boy going up to the steamboat, right through to where she hugged the king at the front door. Mary Jane's face was afire, like sunset.

"Well," I said, "it's a rough gang, these two frauds, and I'm fixed so I got to travel with them a while longer, whether I want to or not – I'd rather not tell you why. There is another person for you on a piece of paper, and you can read it along the road to Mr. Lothrop's, if you want to. Do you reckon that'll do?"

"Oh, yes."

So I wrote, "I put it in the coffin. It was in there when you were crying there, away in the night. I was behind the door, and I was mighty sorry for you, Miss Mary Jane."

Then she shook me by the hand, hard, and said, "GOOD-bye. I'm going to do everything just as you've told me; and if I don't ever see you again, I shan't ever forget you. And I'll think of you many, many a times, and I'll PRAY for you, too!"

And she was gone.

Towards the end of the afternoon, the two rogues were having a public auction of the Wilks' property. By and by everything was sold – everything but a little old trifling lot in the graveyard. It was like the king wanted to swallow EVERYTHING.

that you don't know about who'd be in big trouble. Well, we got to save HIM, haven't we?"

Saying these words put a good idea in my head. I saw how maybe I could get me and Jim rid of the frauds; get them jailed here, and then leave. I said, "Miss Mary Jane, I'll tell you what we'll do. Is there any place a little out of town, where you could go and stay three or four days?"

"Yes; Mr. Lothrop's."

"Well, that'll do. Now you go along out there, and lay low till nine or half-past to-night, and then ask them to bring you home again. If you get here before eleven, put a candle in this window; if I don't turn up wait till eleven; and then if I don't turn up it means I've got safely out. Then you can come out and spread the news around, and get these crooks jailed."

"Good," she said, "I'll do it."

Then I said, "I'd rather not TELL you where I put the money, Miss Mary Jane; but I'll write it

Well, while they were at it, a steamboat landed, and in about two minutes a very nice-looking old gentleman, and a nice-looking younger one, with his right arm in a sling came towards the king. That old gentleman looked all puzzled to death.

Pretty soon he turned around to the crowd, and said, "This is a surprise to me; for my brother and me have had misfortunes; he's broke his arm, and our baggage got lost. I am Peter Wilks' brother Harvey, and this is his brother William, who can't hear nor speak. We are who we say we are; and in a day or two, when I get the baggage, I can prove it. But up till then I won't say anything more, but go to the hotel and wait."

So he and his companion went off; and the king laughed, and cried out, "Broke his arm - very convenient! Lost their baggage! That's MIGHTY good! – Under the CIRCUMSTANCES!

So he laughed again; and so did everybody else, except three or four, or maybe half a dozen. One of these was that doctor; another one was a sharp looking gentleman, with a carpet-bag – it was Levi Bell, the lawyer. There was yet another person – a big rough and strong looking man called Hines. And when the king finished his speech, this man went up to him and said, "Say, look here; if you are Harvey Wilks, when'd you come to this town?"

"The day before the funeral, friend," said the king.

"At what time?" said Hines.

"In the evening."

"How did you come?"

"I came down on the steamboat from Cincinnati."

"Then, how did you come to be up at the Pint in the morning – in a canoe?"

"I wasn't up at the Pint in the morning."

"This man is a fraud and a liar," Hines told

the crowd. "He was up at the Pint that morning. I live up there, don't I? I saw him there. He came in a canoe, along with Tim Collins and a boy."

"Would you know the boy again if you were to see him, Hines?" said the doctor.

"I reckon I would. Why, yonder he is, now. I know him perfectly easy."

It was me he pointed at.

The crowd became completely crazy; while we, the king's friends all started.

It was about sundown. The doctor led me along by the hand, and was kind enough, but he never let go my hand. We all got in a big room in the hotel, and lit up some candles, and fetched in the two newcomers.

Pretty soon, the new gentleman broke in, and said, "I've thought of something! Is there anybody here that helped to lay out the late Peter Wilks for burying?"

"Yes," said somebody, "I and Ab Turner did it. We're both here.'

Then the old man turned towards the king, and said, "Perhaps this gentleman can tell me what was tattooed on Peter Wilks' breast?"

The king turned a little white; he couldn't help it! It was pretty still in there, and everybody bent a little forward and gazed at him.

But king was quite a tricky fellow. Pretty soon, he began to smile, and said, "Yes sir, I CAN tell you what was tattooed on his breast. It was just a small, thin, blue arrow."

Well, I never saw anyone like that old trickster having such clean out-and-out cheek!

The new old gentleman turned towards Ab Turner and his mate and said, "There – you've heard what he said! Was there any such mark on Peter Wilks' breast?"

Both men spoke up and said, "No, we saw no such mark."

"Good!" said the old gentleman. "Now, I'll tell you what you DID see on his breast: The initials: P – B – W. Isn't it so?"

Both of them spoke up again, and said, "No, we DIDN'T. We didn't see any marks at all."

Well, everybody WAS in a state of mind now. All began shouting, "All of them are frauds! Let's drop them down from a height! Let's drown them! Let's ride them on a rail!" and everybody was whooping at once, and there was a rattling powwow.

Then the lawyer jumped on the table and yelled, "Gentlemen – gentlemen! Hear a word – just a SINGLE word – if you PLEASE! There's one way yet – let's go and dig up the coffin and see for ourselves."

That took their attention.

"Hooray!" they all shouted.

"Hold on, hold on!" said the lawyer and the doctor, "fetch along these four men and the boy, too!"

"We'll do it!" they all shouted; "and if we don't find the marks we'll lynch the whole gang!" I WAS scared, now, I tell you. But there wasn't any getting away, you know. They gripped us all, and marched us right along, straight for the graveyard, which was a mile and a half down the river, and the whole town at our heels.

As we went by our house I wished I hadn't sent Mary Jane out of town; because if she were here she could tell all and save me.

Well, we swarmed along down the river road, shouting just like wildcats. And to make everything scarier, the sky was darkening up, the lightning beginning to wink and flitter, and the wind to shiver amongst the leaves. This was the most awful and dangerous trouble I ever was in!

Pretty soon, they got into the graveyard and dug and dug like anything. Then it got awfully dark, and began to rain.

But the people never took any notice of it; they were so full of this business.

At last, they got out the coffin and began to unscrew the lid.

All of a sudden, the lightning let go a perfect

glare of white glare, and somebody cried out, "Look, here's the bag of gold on his breast!"

Hines, who was holding my hand, let out a whoop, like everybody else, dropped my wrist and gave a big surge to bust his way in and get a look.

I got my chance. Straight away, I lit out and ran for the road in the dark.

I ran and ran till I reached the town. I saw that there was nobody out in the storm so I walked on through the main street. When I got near our house I looked at it: the house all dark.

But, at last, just as I was sailing by, FLASH comes the light in Mary Jane's window! She was back.

I felt pretty sad at going away from her. However, soon, the house and all was behind me in the dark.

I fairly flew towards the shore. I borrowed a boat that wasn't chained, and set out for the raft. As I sprung aboard the raft, I cried out, "Out with you, Jim, and set her loose! Glory be to goodness, we're free of them!"

Jim rushed out, and came towards me with both arms spread, he was so glad I was back and we were free of the king and the duke.

So, in two seconds, away we went sliding down the river, and it DID seem so good to be free again and all by ourselves on the big river, and nobody to bother us.

Suddenly, I heard a noise. I knew the sound mighty well, and held my breath and listened and waited. And sure enough, when the next flash busted out over the water, I saw the king and the duke making their way towards our raft!

I fell right down on to the planks; and it was all I could do to keep from crying.

WHEN they got aboard, the king came to me, shook me by the collar, and said, "Trying to give us the slip, was you, you pup! Tired of our company, hey?"

And then he shook me up again, and said he

would drown me.

But the duke said, "Let go of the boy, you old idiot! Would YOU have done any differently? Did you inquire around for HIM when you got loose? I don't remember it."

So the king let go of me, and begun to abuse that town and everybody in it.

Then, the king and duke got into an argument about the money. They started accusing each other of stealing the cash and hiding it, especially since they had added the proceeds of the Royal Nonesuch to the pot.

The duke finally grew very angry and attacked the king.

"Take your hands off! – let go my throat!" cried the king. "You got to SAY you did it, or..." said the duke.

The king began to gurgle, and then he gasped out, "No! - I OWN UP!"

I was very glad to hear him say that; it made me feel much easier than what I was feeling before. So the duke took his hands off and said, "If you ever deny it again I'll drown you."

The king said, timidly, and still snuffling, "Why, duke, it was you that said make up the deficit; it wasn't me."

"Stop crying! I don't want to hear anything more!" said the duke.

So the king sneaked into the tent and took to his bottle for comfort, and before long the duke tackled HIS bottle.

And so, in about a half an hour the two men were totally drunk and as thick as thieves again.

CHAPTER 11

Jim Goes Missing

We dared not stop again at any town for days and days; and kept right along down the river. We were down south in the warm weather now, and a mighty long way from home. And at last the two frauds again began to lay their heads together and talk low and confidentially, for hours at a time. Jim and I got uneasy. We judged they were up to some kind of worse devilry than ever.

So then we were pretty scared, and made up an agreement that we wouldn't have anything to do with such acts, and we would clear out and leave them behind at the first chance we got.

Well, early one morning we hid the raft in a good, safe place about two miles below a little shabby village, and the king went ashore. But midday came and king did not return to the raft. So I and the duke went up to the village, and hunted around there for the king. By and by we found him in the back room of a little low drinking-house. He was quite drunk. The duke too joined him and pretty soon was as drunk as the king. Then he began to abuse him and said he was an old fool. The king too began to abuse back.

The minute they were fairly at it, I lit out and spun down the river road like a deer; for I saw that it was our chance to fly.

I got down to the raft all out of breath but loaded up with joy, and cried out, "Set her loose, Jim! We're all right now!"

But there wasn't any answer, and nobody came out of the tent. I set up a shout—and then another—and then another one; and ran this way and that in the woods, whooping and screeching; but it wasn't any use—old Jim was gone!

Then I sat down and cried; I just couldn't help it.

But I couldn't sit still for long.

Pretty soon, I went out on the road, trying to think what I should do. Then I ran across a boy, and asked him if he'd seen a slave.

"Yes," he said.

"Where?" I said.

"Two miles below, down to Silas Phelps' place; an old fellow had nailed him. He sold out the runaway slave for forty dollars."

Saying this, the lad went off. And I was sure

that it was the doing of the old rogue, the king who had sold Jim and taken the money to get drunk. I went to the raft, and sat down inside the tent to think.

I felt terrible. After all we'd done for those rogues they could have the heart to trick Jim like that, and make him a slave again, and amongst strangers, too; and all for forty dirty dollars.

Then it hit me all of a sudden that the hand of Providence was slapping me in the face for stealing a poor old woman's slave that hadn't ever done me any harm. I felt my wickedness was being watched from above. I almost dropped in my tracks, I was so scared.

Then I got to thinking over our trip down the river; and I could see Jim before me all the time: in the day and in the night-time, sometimes moonlight, sometimes storms, and we floating along, talking and singing and laughing.

I was full of trouble, full as I could be; and didn't know what to do. But then, I made my mind. I would go to work and steal Jim out of slavery again; and if I could think up anything worse, I would do that, too. And if it is wrong; all right, then, I'll GO to hell!

Then I struck up the road, and when I passed the mill I saw a sign on it, "Phelps' Sawmill."

I shoved along, straight for town. When I got there it was all still and Sunday-like. Phelps' was one of these little one-horse cotton plantations. When I got half-way round the farm, a woman came running out of the house. She was about forty-five or fifty years old. Behind her came a brood of small children. She was smiling all over so that she could hardly stand still.

"It's YOU, at last! — isn't it?" she cried.

I said, "Yes ma'am," before I could even think.

The woman grabbed me and hugged me tightly; and then gripped me by both hands and shook and shook. The tears came in her eyes, and ran down over. She kept saying, "You don't look as much like your mother as I reckoned you would. I'm so glad to see you! Children, it's your cousin Tom! — tell him howdy."

But the children ducked their heads, and put their fingers in their mouths, and hid behind her. So then she started for the house, leading me by the hand, and the children tagging after. When we got there she sat me down in a splitbottomed chair, and sat herself down on a little low stool in front of me; then holding both of my hands, she said, "All these long years we have waited for it and it's come at last! We have been expecting you a couple of days and more. What kept you? — Boat got stuck?"

"Yes, ma'am—she—"

"Don't say yes ma'am—say Aunt Sally. Your uncle's been gone to the town to fetch you, not more than an hour ago; he'll be back any minute now."

Mrs Phelps went on and on, asking all sorts of questions. I was getting so uneasy that I wanted to get the children out to one side and pump them a little, and find out who I was. Pretty soon, Mrs Phelps made cold chills streak all down my back, because she said, "You haven't told me a word about Sis. Just tell me about every one of them; and how they are, and what they're doing."

I opened my mouth to begin; but at this point, she grabbed me and hustled me in behind the bed, and said, "Here he comes! Keep silent. I'll play a joke on him. Children, don't you say a word."

I saw I was in a fix now. But there wasn't anything to do but be ready to stand from under when the lightning struck.

When the old gentleman came in, Mrs. Phelps jumped toward him, and said, "Look, its TOM SAWYER!"

By jings, I most slumped through the floor!

The old gentleman grabbed me by the hand and shook, and kept on shaking; and all the time the woman danced around and laughed and cried; and then both fired off questions about Sid, and Mary – Tom Sawyer's siblings, and the rest of the tribe.

But if they were joyful, it was nothing compared to what I was! For it was like being born again, I was so glad to find out who I was. Being Tom Sawyer, my own best friend was easy and comfortable, and it stayed easy and comfortable till, by and by, I heard a steamboat coughing along down the river. Then I said to myself, suppose Tom Sawyer comes down on that boat? And suppose he steps in here any minute, and cries out my name before I can throw him a wink to keep quiet?

Well, it wouldn't do at ALL. I must go up the road and waylay him.

So, I told the folks I reckoned I would go up to the town and fetch my baggage that I had left there. The old gentleman wanted to go along with me; but I said no, I could drive the horse myself, and I'd rather he didn't trouble about me.

So I started for town in the wagon. When I was half-way I saw a wagon coming, and sure enough it was Tom Sawyer. I stopped and waited till he came along.

"Hold on!" I cried, and the wagon stopped alongside. Tom's mouth opened up like a trunk, and stayed so; and he swallowed two or three times like a person that's got a dry throat.

Then, he said, "I haven't ever done you any harm. You know that. So, then, why you want to come back and haunt ME for?"

I said, "I haven't come back—I haven't been GONE."

When he heard my voice it righted him up some, but he wasn't quite satisfied yet. He said, "Honest, you aren't a ghost?"

"Honest, I am not," I said.

"Looky here, weren't you ever murdered AT ALL?"

"No. I wasn't ever murdered at all—I played it on them. You come in here and touch me if you don't believe me." So he did it; and it satisfied him. And he was so glad to see me again he didn't know what to do. And he wanted to know all about it right away, because it was a grand adventure, and mysterious.

But I said, leave it alone till later; and I told him the kind of a fix I was in, and what did he reckon we better do?

He said, let him alone a minute, and don't disturb him. Then he thought and thought, and pretty soon he said, "It's all right; I've got it. Take my trunk in your wagon, and let on it's yours; and then follow me."

"All right; but wait a minute," I said, "There's one more thing—And that is; there's a runaway slave here that I'm atrying to steal out of slavery, and his name is JIM—old Miss Watson's Jim." He said, "What! Why, Jim is..."

He stopped and went back to thinking.

I said, "I know what you'll say. You'll say it's dirty, low down business. But I'm low down; and I'm a-going to steal him, and I want you keep mum and not let on. Will you?"

Tom Sawyer's eye lit up. "I'll HELP you steal him!" he cried.

Well, I got a jolt like I was shot. It was the most astonishing speech I ever heard. Tom Sawyer a SLAVESTEALER!

"Oh, you're joking!" I said.

"I am not joking, either."

In about half an hour Tom's wagon drove up to the front stile, and Aunt Sally saw it through the window.

She said, "Why, somebody has come! I wonder who it is. Why, I do believe it's a stranger."

Everybody made a rush for the front door. Tom was over the stile and starting for the house; we were all bunched in the front door.

He lifted his hat ever so graciously and daintily, like it was the lid of a box that had butterflies asleep in it and he didn't want to disturb them. Then he said, "Mr. Archibald Nichols, I presume?"

"No, my boy," said the old gentleman, "Nichols's place is down a matter of three mile more. But we won't LET you go—it wouldn't be Southern hospitality to do it. Come right in."

"Oh, DO," said Aunt Sally; "You must stay. It's a long, dusty three mile, and we can't let you walk. Come right in and make yourself at home."

So Tom thanked them very handsomely, and came in. When he was in he said he was a stranger from Hicksville, Ohio, and his name was William Thompson—and he made another bow.

Well, he ran on, and on, making up stuff about Hicksville and everybody in it he could invent. I was getting a little nervous, and wondering how this was going to help me out of my scrape. Then, at last, still talking along, Tom reached over and kissed Aunt Sally.

Aunt Sally jumped up and wiped it off with the back of her hand, and cried, "You impudent boy! What do you mean by kissing me?"

Tom looked kind of humble, and said, "Why, I'm sorry, and I wasn't expecting it. They all told me to. But I'm sorry, ma'am, and I won't do it any more—I won't, honest. Tom, (here, he turned toward me) didn't you think Aunt Sally would open out her arms and say, 'Sid Sawyer..."

"Goodness!" said Aunt Sally, breaking in and jumping for him. "You impudent young rogue, to fool a body so ...."

Then she hugged him and kissed him over and over again, and then turned him over to the old man. And after they got a little quiet again, she said, "Why, dear me, I never see such a surprise. Sis never wrote to me about anybody coming but Tom."

"It's because it wasn't INTENDED for any of us to come but Tom," he said; "but I begged and begged, and at the last minute she let me come, too. And then I and Tom thought out this surprise for you."

Pretty soon, we had dinner and there were things enough on that table for seven families—and all hot, too. There was a considerable good deal of talk all the afternoon, and I and Tom were on the lookout all the time; but it wasn't of any use: they didn't happen to say anything about any runaway slave.

CHAPTER 12

Rescuing Jim

That night after supper, Tom and I went to our room, climbed out of the window and down the lightning-rod, and shoved for the town. On the road, Tom told me all about how it was reckoned I was murdered, and how Pap disappeared pretty soon, and didn't come back any more, and what a stir there was when Jim ran away.

Then I told Tom of the raft voyage.

By and by, Tom said, "Looky here, Huck, I bet Jim is in that hut down by the cotton plantations. When we were at dinner, I saw a slave go in there. He unlocked the padlock when he went in, and he locked it again when he came out.

He fetched uncle a key about the time we got up from table."

What a head for just a boy to have! If I had Tom Sawyer's head, I wouldn't trade it off to be a duke, nor mate of a steamboat, nor clown in a circus, nor nothing I can think of.

Pretty soon, Tom told me about his plan. But I needn't tell what it was here, because I knew it wouldn't stay the way it was. I knew Tom would be changing it around every way as we went along, and packing in new tricks wherever he got a chance.

When we got home, the house was all dark and still. So, we went down to the hut by the cotton plantations to examine it. We looked at the front and the two sides; and we found a square window hole, tolerably high, with just one stout board nailed across it.

I said, "Here's the way out. This hole's big enough for Jim to get through if we wrench off the board."

However, Tom thought the plan was just too simple! He wanted a much more complicated and smart plan, and a bit risky too.

Tom said, "I bet we can find a way that's twice as long. We'll DIG him out of a tunnel! It will take about a week!"

Next morning, we were up at the break of day. Then we went down to the slave cabins to pet the dogs and make friends with the slave that fed Jim. He was called Nat, and he was a good natured, woolly haired fellow. Tom coaxed Nat to take us to the captive slave. He told Nat that we hadn't ever seen a runaway slave and were sort of curious to see one. Nat agreed.

Jim was mighty surprised to find Tom and me. He almost shouted in joy. But Tom and I winked at him to keep mum as Nat had gone just for a while. Tom whispered to Jim that we were going to set him free. Jim only had time to grab us by the hand and squeeze it, when Nat came back.

Well, that night, we sneaked out and started digging with our case knives (digging with knives instead of shovels was of course Tom's idea). However, pretty soon we got tired. Our hands got blistered too, and it did not look as if we had done anything at all! Finally, Tom sighed and agreed to use a pick and shovel, so long as we pretended we were using case knives.

The next day, we finished digging the hole.

Jim was so glad to see us again that he almost cried; and called us honey, and all the pet names he could think of. He wanted us to hunt up a cold-chisel to cut the chain off of his leg with right away, and clear out without losing any time. But Tom showed him how irregular it would be! He sat down and told him all about his unbelievable plans, and not to be the least afraid, because we would see he got away, for SURE.

Good old Jim agreed and said it was all right. We sat there and talked over old times for a while, and then Tom asked a lot of questions. Jim told him Uncle Silas came in every day or two to pray with him, and Aunt Sally came in to see if he was comfortable and had plenty to eat, and both of them were kind as they could be.

Then, Tom thought of something new, and said, "You got any spiders in here, Jim?"

"No, thanks to goodness I haven't," said Jim.

"All right, we'll get you some," Tom told him.

"But bless you, I don't WANT any! I'm afraid of them! I'll just soon have rattlesnakes around."

Tom thought a minute or two, and said, "It's a good idea. Where could you keep it?"

"Keep what, Master Tom?"

"Why, a rattlesnake."

"Goodness gracious! Why, if there was a rattlesnake to come in here I'd bust right out through that log wall!"

"Why, Jim, you wouldn't be afraid of it after a little. You could tame it."

"TAME it! PLEASE, Master Tom – DON'T talk so! I can't STAND it!"

"Jim, don't act so foolish. A prisoner's GOT to have some kind of a dumb pet."

But Jim was not glad about it.

So, by and by Tom said, "Well, You got any rats around here?"

"No, I haven't seen any."

"Well, we'll get you some rats."

"Why, Master Tom, I don't WANT any rats."

"But, Jim, you GOT to have them – they all do. Prisoners aren't ever without rats. And they train them, and pet them, and teach them tricks."

Then, Tom waited to think and pretty soon

he said again, "Oh, there's one thing I forgot. Jim, could you raise a flower here?"

"I don't know, but maybe I could, Master Tom."

"Well, you try it, anyway. Some other prisoners have done it. We'll fetch you a little one and you raise it. And then water it with your tears."

"Why, I got plenty spring water, Master Tom."

"No, not spring water; you have to water it with your tears. It's the way they always do."

"She'll die then, Master Tom, she surely will; coz I don't cry."

Tom was stumped. But he studied it over, and then said Jim would have to do the best he could with an onion. He promised he would drop one, in Jim's coffeepot, in the morning.

Jim found everything so very tricky, what with the work and bother of raising the flower, and the rats, and petting and flattering up the snakes and spiders, that it was much more difficult for him to be a prisoner.

Tom lost all patience with him; and said Jim had lost all chances of becoming a celebrated prisoner. Poor Jim said he was sorry, and said he wouldn't behave so any more; and then I and Tom shoved for bed.

CHAPTER 13

Anonymous Letters

Well, by the end of three weeks everything was in pretty good shape.

Then one day, we overheard Uncle Phelps planning that he would advertise in the St. Louis and New Orleans Papers about Jim. I saw that we hadn't any time to lose now. Tom said that now it was time for the anonymous letters.

"What are they?" I said.

"They are warnings to the people that something is up. Sometimes it's done one way, sometimes another."

So Tom wrote the anonymous letter, and I shoved it under the front door, the way Tom told me to.

The letter said:

BEWARE. TROUBLE IS BREWING. KEEP A SHARP LOOKOUT.

– UNKNOWN FRIEND

Next night, we stuck a picture, which Tom drew in blood, of skull and crossbones - on the front door. The next night, we stuck another picture, that of a coffin on the back door.

I never saw a family in such a panic. They couldn't be worse scared. If a door banged, Aunt Sally jumped and said "ouch!" If anything fell, she jumped and said "ouch!" If you happened to touch her, when she wasn't noticing, she did the same. She couldn't turn any direction and be satisfied, because she felt there was something behind her every time.

So the thing was working very well indeed!

Then Tom said, now for the grand bulge!

So, the very next morning at the streak of dawn we got another letter ready.

This letter said:

DON'T BETRAY ME, I WISH TO BE YOUR FRIEND. THERE IS A DESPERATE GANG OF CUT-THROATS GOING TO STEAL YOUR RUNAWAY SLAVE TONIGHT, AND THEY HAVE BEEN TRYING TO SCARE YOU SO AS YOU WILL STAY IN THE HOUSE AND NOT BOTHER THEM. THEY WILL SNEAK DOWN FROM NORTHWARDS, ALONG THE FENCE, AT EXACTLY MIDNIGHT, WITH A FALSE KEY, AND GO IN THE SLAVE'S CABIN TO GET HIM.

–UNKNOWN FRIEND.

After supper that night, we found Uncle Phelps and Aunt Sally in a frightful panic and worry; and they made us go right off to bed the

minute we had done supper.

Tom and I got up about half-past eleven. Then Tom took up Aunt Sally's dress that he stole and was going to start with the lunch, but said, "Where's the butter?"

"We can get along without it," I said.

"We can get along WITH it, too," he said; "you just slide down cellar, fetch it and come along. I'll go and change Jim's clothes to represent his mother in disguise."

So out went Tom, and I went down the cellar. I took up the hunk of butter, blew out my light, and started upstairs very stealthily, and got up to the main floor all right. But here I came across Aunt Sally coming with a candle, and I clapped the food in my hat, and clapped my hat on my head; and the next second she saw me, and said, "You've been down cellar?"

"Yes ma'am."

"What have you been doing down there at this time of night?"

She was in a panic about every little thing right now; so she said, very decidedly, "You just march into that sittingroom and stay there till I come."

Aunt Sally went away, while I opened the door and walked into the sitting-room.

My, there was a crowd there! There were FIFTEEN farmers, and every one of them had a GUN!

I felt terribly sick, and slunk down to a chair.

The farmers were sitting around, and some of them were talking in a low voice. All of them were fidgety and uneasy, but were trying to look like they weren't.

I did wish Aunt Sally would come, and get done with me, and let me get away and tell Tom how we'd overdone this thing. The place was getting hotter and hotter and the butter was beginning to melt and run down my neck and behind my ears; and pretty soon, I was so fidgety that I almost dropped; and a streak of

butter came trickling down my forehead.

Aunt Sally came and saw it. She turned white as a sheet, and said, "What IS the matter with the child? He's surely got the brain-fever, and they're oozing out!"

And she snatched off my hat, and out came what was left of the butter! Then she grabbed me, and hugged me, and said, "Oh, what a turn you did give me! Dear, dear, why didn't you TELL me that was what you'd been down there for, I wouldn't have cared. Now clear out to bed, and don't let me see any more of you till morning!"

I was up stairs in a second and down the lightning rod in another one, and was shinning through the dark for Tom.

When I saw him I could hardly get my words out, I was so anxious. But I told Tom as quickly as I could that we must jump for it now! There was not a minute to lose—the house full of men, with guns!

"Hurry! HURRY!" I said. "Where's Jim?"

"He's dressed, and everything's ready. Now we'll slide out," said Tom.

But then we heard the tramp of men coming to the door, and heard them begin to fumble with the padlock, and heard a man say, "I TOLD you we'd be too soon; they haven't come—the door is locked. Here, some of you lay in the dark and kill them when they come. The rest of you scatter around, and listen if you can hear them coming."

CHAPTER 14

The Flight

So in came the people, but couldn't see us in the dark. Most of them tread on us while we were hustling to get under the bed. But we got under all right, and out through the hole—Jim first, me next, and Tom last.

Now we heard footsteps close by outside.

So we crept to the door, slid out, and stooped down, not breathing, or making any

noise, and slipped stealthily towards the fence in a file. Jim and I got over the fence; but Tom's breeches caught fast on a splinter on the top rail.

Then he heard the steps coming towards him, so he had to pull loose, which snapped the splinter and made a noise.

And as he dropped down to the ground, somebody cried out, "Who's that? Answer or I'll shoot!"

But we didn't answer; we just ran and ran. Then there was a rush, and a BANG, BANG, BANG! And the bullets fairly whizzed around us! We heard them sing out, "Here they are! They've broken for the river! After them, boys, and turn loose the dogs!"

We could hear them because they wore boots and yelled. When they got pretty close on to us we dodged into the bush and let them go by, and then dropped in behind them. Then we whizzed along till we reached where my

canoe was tied. We all hopped in and pulled towards the middle of the river. Then we struck out, easily and comfortably for the island where my raft was; and we could hear the dogs yelling and barking at each other all up and down the bank, till we were so far away the sounds got dim and died out.

And when we stepped on to the raft, I said, "Now, old Jim, you're a free man again, and I bet you won't ever be a slave any more."

We were all glad as we could be, but Tom was the gladdest of all because he had a bullet in the calf of his leg!

Suddenly, I and Jim didn't feel as confident as we did before. The wounded leg was hurting Tom considerably, and bleeding; so we laid him in the tent and tore up one of the duke's shirts to bandage him. But Tom said, "Give me the rags; I can do it myself. Don't stop now; don't fool around here. Boys, we did it elegantly!"

But I and Jim were consulting—and thinking.

And after we'd thought a minute, I said, "Say it, Jim."

So Jim said, "Well then, I won't budge a step out of this place without a DOCTOR!"

I told Tom I was going for a doctor. Tom raised a considerable row about it, but Jim and I stuck to it and didn't budge.

I left for fetching the doctor, telling Jim to hide in the woods when he saw the doctor coming and stay there till he was gone again.

THE doctor was an old man; a very nice, kind-looking old man. I told him that I and my brother were over on Spanish Island hunting. About midnight, my brother must have kicked his gun in his dreams, for it went off and shot him in the leg. I asked the doctor to go over there and fix it and not let anybody know, because we wanted to come home this evening and surprise our folks.

"Who are your folks?" he said.

"The Phelpses."

So the doctor lit up his lantern, and got his saddle-bags, and we started. But when he saw the canoe he didn't like the look of her—said she was big enough for one, but didn't look pretty safe for two. He was not ready to budge in the canoe. So, I had to let him have my canoe and told him just how to find the raft.

I thought that I will wait till the doctor came back. Soon, I fell asleep. When I woke up, the sun was away up over my head! I had overslept! I ran for the doctor's house, but they told me he wasn't home. So I ran and turned the corner, and nearly rammed my head into Uncle Silas' stomach!

He said, "Why, TOM! Where you been all this time, you devil?"

"I haven't been anywhere," I said, "only just hunting for the runaway slave—I and Sid. We followed the men and the dogs, but we lost them. But we thought we heard them on the water, so we got a canoe and went out after

them and crossed over, but couldn't find them. So we cruised along up shore till we got kind of tired and came back. Sid is at the post-office to see what he can hear, and I'm looking to get something to eat for us; and then we were going to come home."

When we got home, Aunt Sally was so glad to see me. She laughed and cried at the same time, and hugged me. And the place was full of farmers and farmers' wives, all talking about the runaway slave and all the exciting events. And when it was late in the day, the people went away.

Aunt Sally fidgeted a lot because Tom wasn't back. She said she'd sit up for him a while anyway, and keep a light burning so he could see it. And then, when I went up to bed she came up with me and brought her candle, and tucked me in. She sat down on the bed and talked with me a long time. She said what a splendid boy Sid was, and kept asking me every now and

then if I reckoned he could have got lost, or hurt, while she wasn't anywhere near him to help.

And then the tears would drip down silently from her eyes, and I would tell her that Sid was all right, and would surely be home in the morning; and she would squeeze my hand, or maybe kiss me, and tell me to say it again, and keep on saying it, because it did her good, and she was in so much trouble.

I felt mean, and I couldn't look her in the face. Then, when she was going away she looked down in my eyes steadily and gently, and said, "The door isn't going to be locked, Tom. But you'll be good, won't you? And you won't go? For my sake."

I WANTED badly enough to go and see Tom; but after that I wouldn't have gone, not for kingdoms. She was on my mind and Tom was on my mind, so I slept very restlessly.

CHAPTER 15

All's Revealed

Uncle Phelps couldn't get any track of Tom; and both he and Aunt Sally sat at the table thinking, and not saying anything, and looking mournful, and their coffee getting cold, and not eating anything.

Suddenly, Aunt Sally jumped up and ran, for she saw something. And so did I.

It was Tom Sawyer on a mattress; and that

old doctor; and Jim, in the calico dress, with his hands tied behind him; and a lot of people.

Aunt Sally flung herself at Tom, crying, "Oh, he's dead, he's dead, I know he's dead!"

At that moment, Tom turned his head a little, and muttered something or other.

Then Aunt Sally flung up her hands, and said, "He's alive, thank God! And that's enough!" She flew for the house to get the bed ready, scattering orders right and left at everybody else.

I followed the men to see what they were going to do with Jim; and the old doctor and Uncle Silas followed after Tom into the house. The men were very huffy. They cursed Jim, and give him a cuff or two on the head once in a while.

But Jim never said anything.

They took him to the same cabin as before, and put his own clothes on him, and chained him again, and chained his hands, too, and both

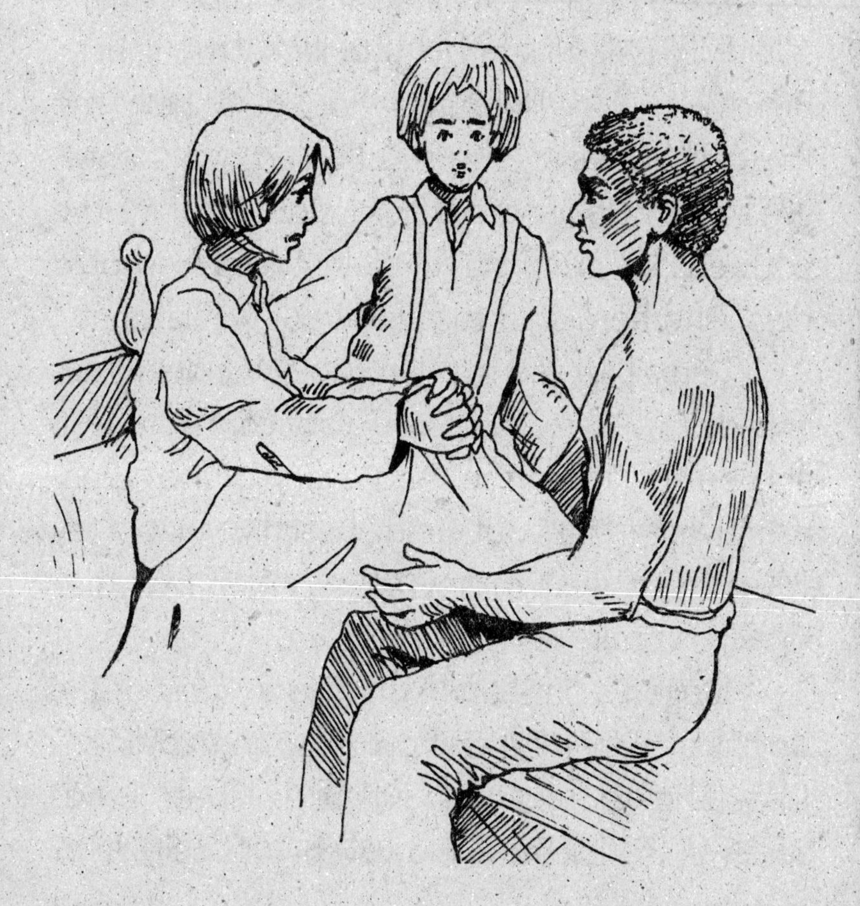

legs. But then, the old doctor came in and said, "Don't be rough on him. He isn't a bad fellow."

The doctor told how Jim had risked his own life and freedom to save the life of Tom.

"When I got to the island, I found that I couldn't remove the boy's bullet without help. But there was nobody who could help me there. Then, feeling helpless I called out, 'If only I got some help!' And, the next moment, this slave crawled out from the forest and said he would help. And he did so too; and very well at that!"

Then all agreed that Jim had acted very well, and deserved to have some notice taken of it, and be rewarded too. And every one of them promised, right out and heartily, that they wouldn't curse him any more. After that they locked him up.

I judged Aunt Sally would soon hear of the doctor's tale. And then how was I to explain my forgetting to mention Sid being shot? I was surely in trouble now. However, Aunt Sally stuck to the sickroom all throughout the day and all the night.

Next morning, I heard Tom was a good deal better. Aunt Sally and I sat near Tom, watching. By and by, he stirred a bit, opened his eyes, and said, "Hello! Why, I'm at HOME! How's that? Where's the raft?"

"It's all right," I said.

"And JIM?"

"The same," I said.

"Good! Splendid! NOW we're all right and safe! Did you tell Aunty?"

Aunty chipped in and said, "About what?"

"Why, about the way the whole thing was done. How we set the runaway slave free—I and Tom."

"What! What IS the child talking about! Dear, dear, is he out of his head again!"

But Tom was so proud and joyful, he just couldn't hold in, and just went on and on about it—Aunty chipping in, and spitting fire all along, and both of them going on and on, all at once, like a cat convention!

Then Aunt Sally said, "WELL, I tell you if I catch you meddling with him again..."

"Meddling with whom?" Tom said, dropping his smile and looking surprised.

"With whom? Why, the runaway slave, of course."

Tom looked at me very gravely, and said, "Tom, didn't you just tell me he was all right? Hasn't he got away?"

"HIM?" said Aunt Sally; "the runaway slave? They've got him back, safe and sound, and he's in that cabin again, on bread and water, and loaded down with chains, till he's claimed or sold!"

Tom rose up in bed, with his eye hot, and his nostrils opening and shutting like gills, and cried out to me, "They have no RIGHT to shut him up! Don't you lose a minute! Turn him loose! He isn't any slave; he's as free as any creature that walked this earth!"

"What DOES the child mean?" said Aunt Sally.

"I mean every word I say, Aunt Sally. Old Miss Watson died two months ago, and she was ashamed she ever was going to sell Jim down the river, and SAID so; and she set him free in her will."

"Then what on earth did YOU want to set him free for, seeing he was already free?" cried Aunt Sally.

"Well, I wanted the ADVENTURE of it!" explained Tom Sawyer.

Aunt Sally was one of the most confused looking persons I ever saw—except one, and that was Uncle Silas. When he came in, they told it all to him. It kind of made him drunk.

We had Jim out of the chains in no time, and when Uncle Silas and Aunt Sally found out how well he helped the doctor nurse Tom, they made a heap of fuss over him, and fixed him up prime, and offered him all he wanted to eat, and gave him nothing to do.

And Tom gave Jim forty dollars for being a prisoner for us, and doing it so nicely.

Jim was pleased almost to death.

And then Tom talked along and said, lets all go for howling adventures over in the Territory, for a couple of weeks or two. I said it was a good idea, but, I hadn't got any money to buy the equipments. I reckon I couldn't get any from home, because Pap must have got it all away from Judge Thatcher and drunk it up.

"No, he hasn't," Tom said; "it's all there yet— six thousand dollars and more; and your Pap hasn't ever been back since."

Then, Jim said in a solemn kind of way, "He isn't coming back any more, Huck."

"Why, Jim?" I asked.

At first, Jim wouldn't tell me. But I kept asking him; so at last he said that the dead man who we found in the floating house was none other but Pap.

Pretty soon, Tom got well. He had his bullet around his neck on a watch-guard as a reminder of this adventure. But, I reckon I have to head out for the adventure ahead of the rest, because Aunt Sally says she is going to adopt me and civilize me.

However, I can't stand being adopted and civilized any more. I had been there before and I just couldn't stand it!

The End